**Award-winning science fiction magazine
published in Scotland for the Universe.**

We're supporting

SCOTLAND'S FESTIVAL OF SCIENCE FICTION. FANTASY & HORROR WRITING

and we thank Cymera for supporting us.

ISSN 2059-2590
ISBN 978-1-9993331-8-8

Shoreline of Infinity is available in digital and print editions.
Submissions of fiction, art, reviews, poetry, non-fiction are welcomed: visit
the website to find out how to submit.

www.shorelineofinfinity.com

Publisher
Shoreline of Infinity Publications / The New Curiosity Shop
Edinburgh
Scotland
040620

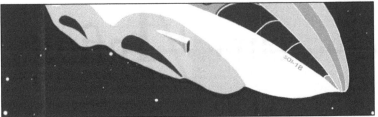

Cover: Jackie Duckworth Art

Contents

**Shoreline of Infinity
Science Fiction Magazine
Editorial Team**

**Guest Editors Tendai Huchi and
Raman Mundair (poetry)**

Co-founder, Editor-in-Chief:
Noel Chidwick

Co-founder, Art Director:
Mark Toner

Deputy Editor & Poetry Editor:
Russell Jones

Reviews Editor:
Samantha Dolan

Non-fiction Editor:
Pippa Goldschmidt

Copy editors:
Iain Maloney, Russell Jones, Pippa
Goldschmidt, Richard Ridgwell

First Contact

www.shorelineofinfinity.com

contact@shorelineofinfinity.com

Twitter: @shoreinf

and on Facebook

Pull up a Log

Can we give a warm welcome to **Raman Mundair** and **Tendai Huchu** our guests editors for *Shoreline of Infinity 18*.

Guest Editors: Tendai Huchu and Raman Mundair

For this issue we turn the spotlight onto BAME science fiction. It was back in December 2019 BC (before COVID-19) when the editorial team, including Tendai and Raman, sat around a table in the Storytelling Centre Café in Edinburgh. With excitement and anticipation we planned this issue, aiming to attract top and new BAME writers from around the world. Take a look at that list of contents over there and you can see how well the guest editors performed; this is a beautiful collection of tales and writings.

This achievement means so much considering all that has happened in the last six months with the effects of the coronavirus on health and society. In the aftermath of the appalling killing of George Floyd, we are watching news and social media reports from the USA, and as I type I have no idea what the world is going to be like when you are reading this.

As the clouds gather perhaps *Shoreline of Infinity 18* can be a tiny beacon for the creative spirit of the human race.

We have a winner!

Congratulations to **Laura Scotland** for winning the (takes deep breath) Cymera, Scotland's Futures Forum and Shoreline of Infinity's Competition for speculative short fiction 2020. The judges describe Laura's story *The Chrysalis* as "emotionally compelling."

—Noel Chidwick, June 2020

Odette

Zen Cho

Odette's time for hope was short.

Early that morning, the first morning of the rest of her life, she'd gone out of her house to the end of the garden. The air was as pure as the breath that first animated the clay of Adam's flesh. She looked out over the island and saw no limitations.

But then she saw him – Uncle Andrew, in his polo shirt and khaki shorts, coming out for his daily morning walk. He pretended not to see her as he opened the gate and passed her by, but he knew she was there.

Odette realised her life had not changed after all. She would have to live with Uncle Andrew for the rest of her life.

He had only died the day before.

Uncle Andrew had insisted on being discharged from hospital.

"If it is my time, I will die with dignity," he said. He spoke slowly, pausing between words to struggle for breath. "A Christian shouldn't be scared of death."

It wasn't Odette's place to disagree. Uncle Andrew's friends from church stepped in for her.

"Andrew, God helps those who help themselves," said Auntie Gladys. "You are still so young. Don't you think it's too soon? Let the doctors treat you."

"God can wait for a while," said Auntie Poh Eng. "He knows how much we all need you!"

All this was no less than what Uncle Andrew expected, but he was inflexible. "The doctors have had their chance. They poke me here, there, everywhere also, they still don't know how to cure me. God is calling me back to Him. I'm not so foolish as to put my faith in humans over God."

Auntie Poh Eng took Uncle Andrew's hand. Her eyes were full of tears.

"God has been good to let us have you for so long," she said.

Auntie Poh Eng was Odette's favourite of their church friends. Her only flaw was an unfailing affection for Uncle Andrew. But this was a flaw shared by all Uncle Andrew's friends. It was not Odette's place to complain.

Her place was by Uncle Andrew's side, except when she was in the laundry room, or the kitchen, or in the dining room polishing the heirloom silver. Just because Uncle Andrew was about to die didn't mean he was about to let standards slip. They had a cleaner who came in every day to go over the house, but the clothes Uncle Andrew wore and the food he ate had to come fresh from Odette's hands. As for the various antiques and other treasures Uncle Andrew had accumulated over the years, they could not of course be entrusted to a cleaner who only earned RM600 a month.

Uncle Andrew had collected enough that looking to the upkeep of his possessions, cooking for him, keeping him in clean clothes and nursing him was too much for one person. Odette suggested that perhaps the cleaner could cook and do the laundry:

"Then I can put hundred per cent into looking after you and the house, Uncle."

"You should already be putting in hundred percent," said Uncle Andrew. "Who is paying for you to live? Not like you have so much to do. When Beatrice was alive she did all this and more. She didn't even have a degree, not like you. She never complained. You young people are spoilt. Given too much."

"Auntie Letchumi is a better cook than me. Maybe you'll feel like eating more, Uncle. It'll be good for your health."

"Instead of learning to cook better, you want to pay someone else to do," said Uncle Andrew. "You're useless! If not for my money I don't know what you'd do – end up lying in the street like a tramp. I don't eat all this Indian food."

"If you don't want her to cook for you, what if we ask her to do the laundry? It will give me more time."

"What else are you doing with your life? Do you have a job? Do you have a husband? All you have to do is take care of your uncle who has done so much for you. Even that you don't want to do. I sacrifice for you and still you are so selfish."

Odette was of the unfortunate mould which does not grow less sensitive with time and use. She fell silent. Crying irritated Uncle Andrew to a fury. He took it as an unjustifiable assertion of self.

"After I die your life will be very easy," said Uncle Andrew. "My time left here is short. But you can't even wait until God takes me." He coughed.

"I'm sorry, Uncle," said Odette.

"There's no use saying sorry," said Uncle Andrew. "You shouldn't be so selfish in the first place. If your hand causes you to sin, cut it off."

He banged the bedside table, but though Odette jumped she wasn't really scared. Five years ago the force of the blow would have rocked the table back and forth on its legs. Now Uncle

Andrew was so weak it barely rattled the glass of water Odette had brought him. She watched the surface of the water tremble and go still, and hid a smile.

Uncle Andrew only spoke this way when they were alone. His friends did not see this side of him.

The friends watched Odette bring in meals, give Uncle Andrew his medicine, serve him hot drinks, fluff his pillow. They didn't see her change his bedsheets every day, bathe and dress him, do the laundry, eat only in the brief intervals granted her between chores – standing at the kitchen counter, stuffing the food into her mouth, dry-eyed.

Auntie Poh Eng told her:

"You are taking Jesus' life as your model. Life is hard now, but God will reward you in the end."

Odette only shook her head. "I don't need His reward, Auntie."

After all, Uncle Andrew had always been so kind to her. He was known for his kindness. A pillar of the church, counsellor to his friends, benign dispenser of advice to their children.

It was all the more impressive in one who had done so well for himself. *Look at that beautiful house he lives in*, said his friends. *In the foothills overlooking the sea.* The only tragedy in Uncle Andrew's life was that he had no children of his own. But then, he had Odette.

To Odette his kindness had been wearyingly comprehensive. It had covered sending her to university, and insisting that she stay in his home for the duration of her course. He never asked for rent – she wouldn't have been able to pay it. In return for accommodation she did the household chores.

She hadn't minded staying at home for university. It had meant living with Uncle Andrew, but she was used to that. The house was almost enough to make up for it.

It was the mansion of a nineteenth-century Peranakan merchant. Uncle Andrew liked to give out, and seemed to half-believe, that it had been in the family for generations, but he

8

had bought it when he was in his forties from the businessman's great-grandson.

"Fella said he's an artist." Uncle Andrew snorted. "Cannot even hold on to the house his father gave him."

Whatever he had been, the great-grandson had had an eye for beauty. Upon Uncle Andrew's arrival the house was exquisitely preserved. No incongruity had been permitted in it, no disruption to its elegant lines.

Uncle Andrew had improved the plumbing and installed air conditioners in every room. He filled the house with big ugly imitations of Western masterpieces, ludicrous photos of himself and Auntie Beatrice, and imposing jade sculptures he bought on trips to China ("I haggled them down to RM500 from RM3,000. These Chinamen will skin you if you don't watch out"). He replaced the Victorian tile flooring with marble, and brought in white leather sofas and glass coffee tables.

But the bones of the house shone through these embellishments. Odette loved the graceful shuttered windows, the intricate latticed vents, the pillars topped with carvings of cranes and fruit. The very gutters were wonderful because they fit so well with the building: they had that perfection that comes from being impeccably appropriate. The beauty and intricacy of the house was such that it could sustain even the incongruity of Uncle Andrew's additions and turn them into something marvellous.

The house was the only thing Odette loved. It was worth staying for.

She'd made the mistake of trying to leave once. Right after she graduated from university Auntie Beatrice died. It was sudden – cardiac arrest, the doctors said.

Odette understood that her aunt had finally given up.

She had not known Auntie Beatrice well, though they had lived under the same roof for many years. Auntie Beatrice had compacted herself so efficiently she seemed to take up no space in the world. Two days after her death Odette found herself struggling to remember what her aunt's face looked like.

Odette had started applying for jobs with a sense of foreboding.

When she was offered a teaching job, she was nonplussed. She had not really expected to get a job. But here it was, her ticket to another life. She would be teaching at a tuition centre in Singapore – would be able to pay rent, feed herself, and live without reference to Uncle Andrew.

But there was the house. If Odette took the job, she would have to leave it. She would not see it again. Uncle Andrew had made it clear when she started university that she was not getting a degree so that she could enter the workforce.

"God has been generous," he said. "As long as I live, nobody else in the family will need to work."

Odette struggled with her decision for days. A week after she'd received the offer, she woke up suddenly in the middle of the night.

Uncle Andrew's bedroom was air-conditioned, but Odette wasn't allowed to turn on the air conditioner in hers – the expense of it. The windows were open and outside the cicadas were shrieking insistently. The mosquito coil burning under her bed scented the air. Moonlight shone through the air vents high in the walls. Seeing the inky tracery of the shadows cast on the floor, Odette felt a shock of love.

In Singapore it would be an ugly little flat she lived in – bare of flourishes, with grilles on the windows and white fluorescent lighting. She would sit on a cheap sofa from IKEA and watch TV. She would have surrendered the glories of carved ivory and old rosewood armoires in favour of that cold idol, freedom.

Odette went back to sleep with her mind made up.

The next morning Uncle Andrew was waiting for Odette when she came back from the wet market with the groceries. A letter was on the table in front of him.

"All the money I spent on you, and you go and do this?" said Uncle Andrew. "I treat you like my own daughter. Fed you since you were small. Paid for you to go to uni. Someone like you, you think you would have this kind of lifestyle if I didn't pay for you?"

Odette's voice came out strangely calm. "I thought if I get a job, I can be less of a burden on you, Uncle."

"So clever to make excuses now, hah?" said Uncle Andrew. His face had gone dark red. He slammed the table. The letter fluttered. "Don't try to lie to me. You want to run off! Sick of listening to your uncle, is it?"

A prickling sensation spread up Odette's nose and behind her eyes. "I'm sorry I didn't tell you. I forgot."

"You think I'm stupid?" roared Uncle Andrew. "Useless! Idiot! If you're so rushed to get out of this house, get out! Go pack your things and get out! If you don't even know how to be grateful, why should I spend any more money on you? Go lah! Go!"

Odette was sobbing. "Uncle, I just wanted to contribute. I'm ashamed to keep taking your money. I'm an adult already."

"You think I'm the kind of person who won't support their own niece?" said Uncle Andrew. "My friends will be very surprised to hear that. You ask the church people, my staff. Everybody will say Andrew Teoh isn't afraid to spend money on his family. You know better than all these people, is it?"

Odette shook her head. "I was going to reject the offer, Uncle."

"Nice story," said Uncle Andrew. "What for you go and apply then?"

The house gave her the right thing to say.

"I wanted to try," said Odette. "But when they offered, I knew I couldn't accept. I don't want to leave this house."

Uncle Andrew stared at her. The colour in his face faded to pink.

"Hmph," he said. He crumpled the letter and threw it at her. It hit Odette on the shoulder and fell to the floor.

"I don't want to see that again," said Uncle Andrew. "Go put the food in the fridge."

After this, a merciful blankness descended on Odette. She felt nothing, and could even laugh at a couple of Uncle Andrew's jokes at dinner.

The next morning at church, Uncle Andrew sent Odette to the car a couple of times – first for a packet of tissues, then for a copy of a magazine he'd promised Auntie Gladys. When Odette came back with the *Reader's Digest*, Auntie Gladys said:

"So guai your niece, Andrew. If my daughter was so helpful I'll be very happy."

"Beatrice and I did our best to bring her up," Uncle Andrew said. "But what's the most we can do, a childless couple like us?"

"You've done better than so many parents. Odette is lucky to have you all to look after her."

Uncle Andrew inclined his head. "As long as I'm alive, she'll always have a home."

They turned their eyes on Odette – Auntie Gladys's face distant and tender with thoughts of her daughter in America, Uncle Andrew looking just past Odette's ear. She smiled as expected.

When she got home she shut the door to her room and crawled into bed. Her body was sour with hatred. Her eyes burnt with tears.

The house absorbed them – weathered her storm – until she lay boneless on her bed and saw love shine through the vents, as it had done the night she decided to stay.

Odette had been young when her parents died. She didn't miss them as people – more as symbols of a warmth locked in the past, rendered forever inaccessible by their deaths.

Her mother's family were numerous, but lived in Indonesia. Though only a cousin of her father, Uncle Andrew staked his claim before any of her other relatives arrived on the scene. God had been good to them, he said, and he and Beatrice had never intended to waste their good fortune on themselves. Beatrice would enjoy having someone to fuss over. She regretted the fact that they had no children. Uncle Andrew made out that his wife had been the prime mover behind their offer to adopt Odette.

Even then Odette had found this hard to believe. Auntie Beatrice was the quietest woman she had ever met. She never looked up. She spoke in a whisper. It was hard to imagine her daring to want anything.

Uncle Andrew, on the other hand, impressed Odette with unfavourable force. She was still at an age where she only understood snatches of what grown-ups said to her. She watched his face instead of listening to his words, and what she saw worried her.

Two weeks after her parents' death, she was dozing in the back seat of his car as it wound up the hill towards his home.

She always remembered her first sight of the house. Auntie Beatrice had bored her and Uncle Andrew frightened her, but she knew the house to be a friend the moment she laid eyes on it.

How blue it had looked against the green velvet backdrop of the forest – the intense blue of the sea in paintings of summer days. The red tiles on its roof reflected the last of the setting sun; the lanterns hung under the eaves cast a golden glow over the deepening twilight. As she passed through its double doors her skin prickled with the shivery, delightful excitement of being on holiday.

She was given a teak bed with white linen sheets and a headboard carved with peacocks. She slept soundly for the first time since her parents had died.

The house had been made to be loved, but what lived in it was not a real family.

Odette was the only person who knew what the house wanted. Uncle Andrew brooded over his possessions, indulged in tantrums, and tended his public persona as though it was a bonsai. Auntie Beatrice floated through the rooms, never denting a cushion or ruffling a rug.

But Odette divined the house's secrets. Nooks under staircases and crannies between sofas and walls, the perfect size for an eight-year-old to daydream in. Columns of light that moved around the house, picking whatever room suited their fancy. Wistful silences lying in wait in the concrete-floored courtyard, open to the sky.

She watched birds build their nests in the eaves and spiders construct webs in forgotten corners. She knew the moods of the house as well as she knew Uncle Andrew's.

This made her life easier, as Uncle Andrew's moods made her life harder. The house comforted her when Uncle Andrew tore up her homework, upbraided her for her stupidity and ugliness, told her she should have died when her parents did, that he never should have taken her in.

It was not so bad living with Uncle Andrew. Other children got beaten. Other children had nothing to eat. Uncle Andrew usually aimed to miss. He gave her food and clothing and even gifts at birthdays and Christmases. She didn't know how to articulate what was wrong until she heard a stranger's offhand remark.

"I always forget how beautiful your house is, Andrew," said one of his friends. "It's made for peace."

Odette looked past the friend at Uncle Andrew's smiling face. Uncle Andrew did not know or want peace, in a house made for peace. He desecrated it by living there. She had not hated him before that moment.

She didn't cry whenUncle Andrew told her she would have to find somewhere else to live.

"I looked after you long enough already," he said. "People your age are married, have their own house, children! I've done my part. If by now you haven't found a husband, you can only blame yourself."

Uncle Andrew was moving to Singapore.

"I have a lot of friends there, and I know the pastor of my new church," he told Auntie Poh Eng and the rest. "As a Christian in Malaysia, you never know... In Singapore the lifestyle is more convenient. An old man like me, I cannot be driving myself around forever. This Odette never learnt, she's too scared to go on the roads. In Singapore at least you can rely on public transport, not like here."

Odette had not been allowed to learn to drive. She was 31 and she had never had a job.

"Odette will like it," said Auntie Poh Eng, smiling at her. "Singapore is nice for young people. More fun, yes?"

"Ah, Odette won't be coming with me," said Uncle Andrew. "So boring for her to live with an old man. She's going to find her own place. These young people want to be independent. You give them your sweat and blood and at the end of the day, they go off and do what they want."

"That's the way of life," said Auntie Gladys. "But what are you going to do with the house, Andrew? Are you keeping it? It's been in your family for so long."

Uncle Andrew shook his head. "Selling. My grandfather would be upset, but things have changed since his day. A big old house, you must spend so much for upkeep. I'm not earning anymore. I don't want to worry about it in my old age. There's a developer who's very interested. Not many heritage buildings around that are so well-preserved. He wants to turn it into a hotel. The Mat Salleh like all this kind of thing."

Most of the friends nodded, but Auntie Poh Eng looked at Uncle Andrew as if for the first time her belief in him had wavered.

"You're selling to a developer?" she said. "To make it into a hotel?" But she remembered herself almost at once. "Of course most people cannot afford such a beautiful house. Maybe it's nice for them to have the chance to stay here also, even if it's for one or two nights only."

"I haven't answered the developer yet. I'm hoping to find someone who wants to live here," said Uncle Andrew smoothly. "It's very sad to have a home turned into something commercialised. Next best thing would be if the government buys it. Make it into a museum for everybody to visit."

Auntie Poh Eng beamed, her belief in Uncle Andrew restored.

"That would be perfect," she said.

It wasn't Odette's idea. She was standing in the kitchen wiping her hands when she saw a strand of hair on the countertop.

Hair in his food was the greatest sin anyone could commit against Uncle Andrew. Odette picked up the strand of hair and put it in the bin.

The idea was given to her.

Odette already knew Uncle Andrew's birth date. It was easy to find out the time. He kept his birth certificate in the second drawer of the desk in his study, along with his passport and IC.

It was easy, too, to get strands of his hair. She peeled them off his pillows and dug them out of the drain in the shower. She was unflinching in her preparations. She gathered fingernail clippings and even saved a scab he'd picked at absently and discarded on one of the ugly coffee tables.

She'd never done magic before, but she knew how it was done. You went into all that was too close, too sticky, the things human beings didn't share with one another – that was what the hair and fingernails were for. You did it with strong love or strong hatred.

She poured malice into Uncle Andrew, a patient poison that impregnated the food he ate and released fumes into the air he breathed. And it worked. He sickened. His breath grew short and he could no longer enjoy his meals. He became thin and weak and his body was racked with pain.

The doctors said it was cancer, but Odette knew what was killing him. Sometimes she was even a little afraid of the house.

The manner in which Uncle Andrew chose to depart this life was appropriately Victorian. It was a still hot afternoon and Odette was refilling his glass of water when he opened his eyes and said:

"Jesus is calling me."

Odette paused with the glass in her hand, unsure of how to respond.

"Do you want a drink, Uncle?" she ventured.

"Sit down, girl," snapped Uncle Andrew. "People are dying and you still want to do housework. Remember, Mary, not Martha, was praised by the Lord."

Odette sat down. Uncle Andrew was still speaking, more to himself than to her.

"I'm still young. If not for this cancer, I could have been useful to my fellow men for many years. But His will be done. In Heaven," he added contemplatively, "I will see Beatrice again."

It wasn't clear whether the prospect gave him any pleasure.

Odette felt called upon to fill the gap left by the absence of his friends.

"Don't talk like that, Uncle," she said. "There's still hope. The doctor said –"

"Doctors! What do doctors know?" said Uncle Andrew. "Of course there's still hope. What is better than the hope of the Kingdom of Heaven? I have nothing to reproach myself with."

His wandering eyes settled on her with some of their former keenness.

"Nothing," he repeated. "Will you be able to give the account of yourself to Him that I will be able to give? Look into your conscience. Ask yourself."

Odette stayed silent, but she could not help a quick intake of breath then. She was so close.

"Hah," said Uncle Andrew triumphantly. "You see! Look to yourself! Look to yourself before it's too late!"

He didn't die then – only later, after his shouting had sent him into a coughing fit and Odette had given him water and been snarled at for spilling some on him. Finding fault with her put him in such a good mood that he went to sleep with little trouble after that. The next morning Odette found him cold in his bed.

When Uncle Andrew had realised he was dying he'd willed the house to the church. Odette would get a legacy – an annuity of RM8,000 a year.

"More than a lot of people earn by their own hard work," said Uncle Andrew. "You are lucky."

Odette agreed with Uncle Andrew that this was generous. She resented him no more for this than for anything else, though the bulk of his wealth would go to a successful nephew in Canada who hadn't visited in years.

"Jit Beng has children," said Uncle Andrew.

Jit Beng had an Ivy League degree and a big job in a multinational company. Uncle Andrew yearned over Jit Beng with a stifled affection he had never shown his wife or Odette.

Odette didn't care about the money. It was the house she wanted, and it was easy enough to alter the will. She was the one who had filled out the blanks while Uncle Andrew dictated. She'd bought the will-making kit for him from a bookshop. Uncle Andrew didn't believe in lawyers.

Nobody questioned the result. Everyone except Uncle Andrew had thought Odette should get the house. The church got the RM8,000 a year, a generous donation from a faithful servant of the Lord.

Even Jit Beng got something. Odette willed him a kamcheng, part of a Nyonyaware set that had mostly been destroyed when Uncle Andrew had thrown the pieces at her for going to a friend's house after school. She swathed the kamcheng in layers of bubble wrap and posted it to Jit Beng herself.

After the funeral she came home and lay on the chaise longue in the front hall, gazing up at the gorgeous wooden screens that blocked the heat of the sun.

She would have the coffee tables removed. The gigantic TV, that would go. Maybe she could sell it. She'd already put most of the sculptures and paintings away when Uncle Andrew got too ill to come downstairs to see them, but there were a couple she liked and that she would keep.

She would clear away the clutter, give the house space. Let it breathe.

Her eyes were shut, but if she opened them she would see the light shining through her skin, like moonlight through the filigreed vents. For the first time in her life she gave herself up to happiness.

Uncle Andrew walked his usual route. Down the driveway, up the slope to the top of the hill, then back down again to the back gate, where he let himself in.

Odette had been standing by the pillars at the entrance, waiting for him. Her hand curled around a pillar, drawing strength from the house. Perhaps she hadn't really seen him, she told herself. He wouldn't come back. She had just imagined it.

She knew this was a lie. It was not a surprise to see him return. When he lifted the latch on the gate, the sunlight shone through his arm.

If he had been alive she would have felt the movement of air on her skin as he walked past her. He didn't so much as glance at her, though he knew she was there. Temper held him, its weight crumpling his forehead, pulling his mouth taut.

He would be silent for days, pointedly ignoring her in his pique. His anger would fill the house like dark oily smoke. The stench would get into everything.

Life would be the same as it had always been.

Odette saw that the house needed Uncle Andrew more than it loved her. It needed him as much, perhaps, as she did. It would never let either of them go.

The harsh glare of the sun hurt her eyes. It was too hot to be outside. She let go of the pillar and saw that a splinter had driven itself into her palm.

She turned and went into the house. The shade enveloped her, cool as the air in a crypt. The doors swung shut, closing her in.

Zen Cho was born and raised in Malaysia, and lives in the UK. She is the author of the *Sorcerer to the Crown* novels and a novella, *The Order of the Pure Moon Reflected in Water*, as well as the short-story collection *Spirits Abroad*.

You can listen to Zen reading an extract from Odette at
www.shorelineofinfinity.com/zen-cho-reads-from-odette/

Mobay Woods

K. M. McKenzie

The women in our family never live past sixty.

The math's easy to do – count the names going back twelve generations to when the first of us arrived in Mobay Woods.

Mama said it was a weird thing and not to think about it too much. Papa said someone down the line pissed off the devil. Mama said he was stupid.

Mobay Woods made the rules.

The connection between my family and the forty acres of woods that spread out around our house was never explored.

Granny had called our bond, a "sense." We gave to it and it gave to us, and when our lives ended, it took our bodies.

Mobay Woods was the final resting place for all Perry women. Cousin Jenny died on the front porch. Mama cussed out her corpse, letting her body stink for a week. Papa had woken up in the middle of the night, terrified that wild dogs were chewing the flesh off her. Papa had argued about what Jenny did to deserve this treatment. Mama had reminded him of the article she had written about Mobay Woods that nearly ruined the sanctity of the family's sacred place.

Mama, at fifty-eight, had reached the end of her years. Papa was waiting when I walked up to the front porch, stepping foot on property I hadn't been on since I was nineteen, some fifteen years ago. I had always found some excuse not to come home. My three most convincing were a boyfriend, a girlfriend, or work. None really got to the heart of the matter of why I stayed away.

Mama resented me for leaving, but I'd been dogged by the determination to become more than another Perry woman.

"Evangeline," Papa hugged me. "She not doing so good." Papa's voice was deeply grieved, craggier than I had heard it in the past.

Mama was sweating and turning in bed, clinging to a mortuary rock. The Perry women clung to the black quartz from the Mobay Woods instead of crosses and rosaries.

Mama's chest moved up and down and she wheezed. She still looked like Mama, unchanged from when I last saw her over a decade ago. This was another Perry woman trait.

Our skin didn't wrinkle, nor did we grey. Our years, maturity and wisdom flourished entirely in our eyes and voice. We were an anomaly. Been here since the days of slavery, runaways who never got captured, but lived in the backwoods.

"No need to leave. Everything we need is here. As long as we nurture the land, it will keep us," Granny had said.

With the rock in my own hand, I squeezed Mama's hand, rough from years of physical chores.

"Evie," she murmured my name.

I pulled a chair, and sat down to watch her small body crumple on the bed.

"Evie," Mama said again, clamping down on my hand so tightly, I questioned, just for a moment, if she'd gotten her strength back. But her eyes wouldn't even open. She took so long to speak I leaned forward, just to make sure she was breathing.

"There's a reason we die young," she said at last.

"Mama," I tried to tell her she didn't have to explain, but she was already speaking: "We bargained with the woods."

"It's not the woods," I said, almost desperately.

She shook her head weakly, "It's in our blood."

Papa wouldn't hear me out about bringing Mama to seek modern medicine. "It's against her wishes," he said. Perry women didn't like modern medicine. We refused trained doctors and hospitals. Granny nearly lost Mama to foster care because of her refusal to seek treatment in a hospital. My colds, flus and fevers were treated by ointment from plants that grew in Mobay Woods.

When I pushed Papa on the topic, he pushed back: "You forget who you are."

I resented those words. All my life I was torn between my Perry identity and belonging to the world. Mama allowed me to attend regular schools, but barred me from inviting anyone home. Mama wouldn't allow modern technology to grip its tentacles into us. It all drove me mad, defiant. When I got the chance to run away, far away, I did, and never came back until now.

Mama took her last breath that night. I didn't cry, but walked out to the back porch to smoke, only to be surprised when a wooden chair to the right of me squeaked. Papa was sitting there, weeping.

After a short silence, I said, "Can you tell me what she valued?"

"You're a Perry woman, Evangeline," he said coolly.

I was following three generations of broken mother–daughter relationships, but I couldn't recall Mama struggling to find something precious to bury her mama with, no matter how much they hated each other. There was something I had lost, something amiss, after fifteen years away, a kind of ripping of the soul. The fact that I couldn't figure it out, couldn't understand what my mother valued was an indictment on my identity.

"If you can't find it, ask the woods," Papa said, as he wandered into the house.

My eyes fell on Mobay Woods, lush and thick. Something about the woods turned people off. Mama wouldn't hear it about the rumors, and there were plenty. Maybe part of my resentment about this legacy was that I feared I could never truly love and care for the woods the way Mama did.

The child I used to be laughed from deep down inside of me, reminding me of all the fun I used to have in these woods – running, skipping, hide and seek. How could I ever be afraid of it? I could not find a reason now, and realized my fears were foolish. These woods nurtured me as a child, nurtured all of us Perry women. I would return the favor. Imbued with renewed wonderment, a desire to be a part of this great tradition, I stepped off the porch and wandered into the woods, deep into the moonless night. My thick sweater couldn't protect me from the chill.

The quietness got to me. There were almost no animals in the woods. Mama and Granny used chirps, whistling and other sounds that imitated whatever animal they sought – deer, pig, bird. My ears were open. The familiarity of the land washed over me in the cold breeze. Little things, like Papa and me going into the woods to cut lumber that he used to make furniture and toys, drummed to life in my memory.

I remembered, too, the last stranger we allowed here to study our trees. I was fifteen. He was a researcher and environmentalist named Neil Morgan. Mama liked him, and she and Papa weren't in good shape. She knew more about the plants and trees but had let him explain about them scientifically. He had been seeking rare plants and claimed some of the trees were new species. Mama wouldn't let him take samples.

We were the only ones allowed to take from the woods.

I spent time with the researcher here. He had expressed surprise at a crawling snake tree, and had asked me what we called it. He was always taking notes.

Mobay Woods had towering trees and thick green shrubs, and the floor was all undergrowth that made it more like a jungle. The clearing was the place we sought guidance. A hanging tree, a twisting thing with branches that intertwined, marked the clearing.

My brain fought and denied me the invocation of maternal rituals witnessed, of what Granny and Mama would do when they needed help. I resorted to bloodletting and walked to a thorny tree, using its thin vine to poke my inner wrist. A trickle of blood seeped out. The vines of the tree slithered with my touch. It responded to my blood. The scent of goa, a leafy, lavender-type fragrance, saturated the clearing, seeping from the trees.

It came fast, everywhere.

I closed my eyes, and waited through the light-headedness, the whirring unease of the woodland, and the deepening cold and green mist that washed over the clearing.

In my moment of silence, I remembered I was a Perry woman, and my thoughts filled with childhood memories – picking berries, sorting plants, feeding chickens, washing herbs. It was all there, and so was the truth about my mother.

The thing she valued was stored under a floorboard in the closet of her bedroom. A journal. The book was filled with drawings of plants, and a few had scientific name equivalents, not all. It took me a second to realize the notebook wasn't Mama's. Written on the inner back cover was the name of the environmentalist, Neil Morgan.

Mama had said he left abruptly.

This discovery was heart-wrenching.

I returned to the floorboard in the closet and found other things – other journals, a keychain with car and other keys, and a pile of cash. There was also a pair of pristine red baby shoes, tied together with a ribbon. I studied them, confused by their presence. This was Mama's hiding place, but why would she have these? They could've been mine – I believed they were. When I flipped the small, lacy shoes, something fell out from inside of one of them. Neatly folded paper tied with a ribbon.

The folded paper was soft. Slowly, I unraveled its content – a knot of hair intertwined with goa and ukupa leaves, a mixture Granny had called the elixir of life. It was heart medicine.

Mama and Granny used to sell herbal remedies. When disease spread through the county back in great-great-granny's day, our livestock survived, and the town got to talking.

The authorities came to investigate. The town accused my great-granny of witchcraft. It was a great feat that our property hadn't been seized, though in hindsight no one wanted to mess with the Mobay witches.

Mama wrote my name on the paper. She cherished this.

My best guess of what these baby shoes meant – a gris-gris. Granny had made a similar bundle when Mama was a sickly baby.

"Did you know about this?" I asked, finding Papa in the kitchen, sipping gungu latte.

"I have never seen that before."

"Okay, I think I found what mama cherished."

We bury our dead between twelve and one in the morning, when the land was settled. Papa and I carried Mama's body to the woods. Mama said our bodies nurtured the earth in death as it nurtured us in life. There was no digging, just a natural giving to the land. We placed Mama's body down in the shrubs, attaching the baby shoes to it, and waiting for the woods to take it.

Papa left me alone for the last part. It was the way it worked. It was up to me as a woman to see that the land properly took my mother. When it was my turn, a daughter I had yet to decide about having, would do the same for me. There was a sadness knowing I might be the last of the Perry women. In a way, it seemed right. This legacy was never one I was okay with, the reason I had run away. Yet, now that I was here, it seemed ripe for re-examination.

My mother's body vanished within the hour, devoured by the shrubs. When I entered the house, Papa was waiting up for me, a bottle of home-grown wine sitting before him on the kitchen table. We drank.

"How did you meet Mama, anyway?"

He smiled. "I was a runaway slave."

Papa had a sense of humor and I laughed.

"You don't believe me." Papa's eyes were bright as a bulb.

"Okay. Pa, slavery ended in…"

"1865."

"Right. And what year is it?"

"2019."

"So, you're not a runaway slave."

"I was. I escaped from a plantation in North Carolina." He paused a moment. "I was lost in the Woods. Then I heard that woman threatening to shoot me. I threw my hands up quick. She didn't look like she was going to spare me but she asked me questions and she was okay with my answers. Here I was."

"How does what you told me make sense?"

I was the skeptic in the family, who'd run away from the superstition, ashamed of it, and what it meant. Despite this, deep inside, I knew I was in denial of some truth. Mobay Woods was unsettling. I could feel, smell, and hear it.

Papa shrugged, and chugged the wine again. "I was the first man to come from the Woods. But you see, all kinds of people come from it – children, too, babies especially. All your family come from it." He locked eyes with me when he spoke the next sentence. "You should return to the woods at dawn. See what you find."

"What would I find?"

He shrugged and chugged, and then stood. "I am tired."

I struggled to sleep. His words tattooed themselves to my conscience. My family's ties to the Mobay Woods had felt tenuous, wrapped in myth and lore. Never had I believed the woods were anything more than an overgrown grove that my family tended generationally. If what my Papa said was true, and I had little reason to think he lied, then there was some credence to the belief that the woods were sacred, special, and dared I admit it, supernatural.

An inkling startled me on the onset of dawn, a desire to be awake. Papa's words were fresh in my mind, and so I set out to the woods. It had misted up overnight, emanating a fragrant scent that was unique to it.

Walking through the green mist, my ears filled with voices that grew steadily in the distance. I had never walked the length of the woods, and Papa had claimed it was expanding, but not as our neighbor had assumed. The physical boundaries were the same, but it felt bigger when inside of it.

Back when there were more of us Perry women alive, Granny, Mama, and our cousins used to come out to sing and give thanks.

We did it twice a year. The sounds filling my ears reminded me of those times, and I half-expected to see Granny and Mama when I broke through the mist.

The woods lost their familiarity, becoming new. The clearing was bigger and longer than any open space in Mobay Woods. Minutes of walking and careful observation revealed a virgin land.

I ascended a hill, and came across a wooden house, similar to our own Perry house with its rudimentary cuts, built upon generationally. The only things modern about our house were the toilet and the sink, made of bricks and wood instead of steel and porcelain.

The sound of women's voices rung out from the house. I was so taken by this that I started to shake, nervous about who these women were, all the while knowing exactly who they could only be. My breath grew shallower the closer I got to the wooden door, which looked very much like our own. I stopped to listen.

Some of these voices were familiar, and yet the one voice I pined for wasn't there, yet it had to be. Had Mama made it?

I lifted my hand to knock, but stopped myself.

The thought that all my relations could be inside this little house felt like the weight of a thousand mountains. Would they know me? Would they welcome me? Would they see a betrayer of their traditions?

The women started singing. I knew this song, I realized, perking up. "Dry weather houses are not worth a cent, and yet we have to pay so much for rent."

Tears streamed down my eyes as the songs of my childhood, folks songs I'd forgotten filled up my ears. How could I have ignored all of this?

I jerked out of my wallowing at the sound of Mama's voice. "Don't be a stranger, come little girl, come to your mama."

She was singing to me – she had to be. Still I couldn't move, stalled by the shame of hiding who I was. I sobbed.

The door squeaked ajar, drawing my attention.

A woman walked out into the open.

Granny, as I remembered her, as I had last seen her.

"Evangeline?" she said, a look of confusion on her wrinkle-free face. She glanced back to the house. "Why have you come?"

"I sent Mama here."

"Yes, I know."

She glanced to the house and so did I. "I cannot let you in. It's against the rules."

"Is this death?"

"In a way, yes, but in a way, no."

I exhaled.

"Evangeline, did your mama tell you?"

"About why we die young?"

We watched each other. I nodded, recalling why I really came. "She had baby shoes in her closet… I attached them to her body. Are they part of the bargain?" I asked.

Granny was quiet, and then her brown eyes locked with mine. "Take the child with you."

"What do you mean?" I pushed.

"You'll see." Granny dashed back into the house, closing the door. A flood of laughter rushed out, short, deep, rich, each harmonizing over one another like music. All of them sounded happy, pure joy. I imagined all of them were inside, generations of Perry women living side by side in the house that Mobay built.

I wanted to join them, but a baby's cries drew me back to the direction from where I had come. Through the mist, I discovered the child lying in the shrubs, where I had left Mama's body. On its feet were the soft red shoes I had tied to Mama. I picked the baby girl up and peered into her eyes, Granny's eyes, Mama's eyes, my own eyes.

I knew the truth. This was where I had come from. Why we had to die, so we could continue generationally.

The woods twitched, a blink-so-fast-you-might-miss-it sort of phenomenon of light. I spotted the researcher standing by the goa tree, just staring at it hopelessly.

Hadn't Mama killed him?

A smile stretched his lips. "Evangeline. It's you." He wandered over. He hadn't aged, not beyond the age he had been back then, late thirties.

"Have you been here the whole time?" I inquired.

"Since this morning. Your mother went to get me some water. She hasn't been back. I cannot find my notebook, either."

Surprised and not surprised, I said, "You should come to the house."

He nodded.

I might never truly understand Mobay Woods. But this baby was mine through and through. These eyes were undeniable. These woods took some time from me and produced life.

Neil didn't believe he had been in the woods for twenty years, that my mother had trapped him there, so he would wait for me; but, each time we stepped into the woods, it introduced us to some new reality of our life – a wedding we didn't recall having, a courtship that started with him introducing himself to me by saying, "You look like some I should know."

I wanted to be angry with Mama, Granny, too. Instead, I focused my energy on raising my daughter. Every morning we headed out to the woods to plant and grow and explore.

She liked to sketch, and soon she had notebooks of plants – my own budding botanist in training.

We Perry women were keepers of the Woods, after all.

Sometimes I swore I heard the voices of Mama, Granny, and the others, but I never ventured too far out, knowing it wasn't my time. But when that day came I would happily take my place among them.

K.M. McKenzie is a Jamaican-Canadian writer from Toronto. Her stories have appeared in the *Strange Economics* anthology, and in upcoming issues of *Polar Borealis* magazine, and CosmicHorror.net.
She freelances as an Editor/Social Media Lead for TdotSpec Publishing.
Find her on Twitter @kmmauthor.

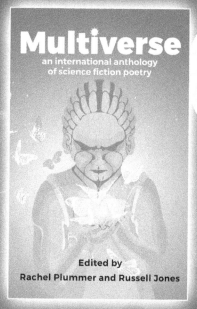

Perumal and the God of Words

Prashanth Srivatsa

"**I**f **the answer is** 'I am my father's third child', what must the question be?"

Perumal hesitated, as he often did in front of the god of words. "I don't know," he muttered after a while.

"Eththanavadhu," the god of words mumbled, the ripple of air deflating, blowing a cloud of bookdust on to Perumal's face as he let go of his knees and coughed. The word, of course, was familiar to him. The question for the answer. Only, it was impossible to translate, and it was the translated phrase the god of words had been anticipating. A playful mockery, no doubt. A sign of his fading strength, slumbering beneath the bookstore, grasping at the echoes of a suppressed tongue.

Perumal felt a tinge of pity, but time was running out. He only knew that the god of words was dying, not how to prevent it.

He scribbled 'eththanavadhu' on a piece of parchment, bowed to the ripple of air and dust, and scrambled up the ladder to the dim lights of the bookstore.

The air above was clammy, books shuttered within cupboards, like warrens with strange powers that ought not be let loose. He rowed past them, past the stacks of magazines and newspapers and to the shutter. Outside, there were not too many people on the streets, yet the distant sound of footfalls was unmistakable. Like cracking earth. By the time he opened the shutter, latched the locks to the wall, and stepped out, a crowd had swarmed in from one end of the lane. Saffron tunics with white and green towels over their shoulders. Betel nuts in their mouths, lips an impatient red. They surrounded a jeep with a man, garbed in white kurta, standing on it. He held a microphone, his voice blaring, forcing heads out of windows, while children scampered out of their homes like he were the ice cream vendor on a blistering April afternoon.

Quietly, Perumal glanced at the shops adjacent to his, at the headboards and at the chalk stands on the verandah with menus and discounts. The Tamil had been erased, replaced by misspelled Hindi names and slogans. A hastily done job, no doubt, but it was not the semantics that bothered him just then. Looking at his own boards, printed in cursive Tamil, he realized he was alone.

The mob carried sticks and stones and, if he squinted a little harder, he could see the glint of black metal poking out behind a cummerbund. Perumal gulped and began to undo the screws of the shutter. Just then, the chemist next door whistled and threw out a piece of chalk on to the sidewalk.

"Quick," she hissed, her head appearing veiled. "Just scratch out the Tamil and scribble something in Hindi. Hurry!"

"That-that's not going to work," Perumal quaked.

The chemist shook her head. "You don't have a choice. They will burn it down."

Perumal thought of the stacks inside, of the poems and the bestsellers he had forced down the other teenagers' throats for his daily rice. He smelled the wood pulp and the calm, floating dust; the whispers of opening lines and the gasps of last chapters. He remembered *Ponniyin Selvan*, the Tamil epic whose last copy he harbored at the deepest trench of his shop, silently reading it under candlelight after sundown.

This is what sedition must feel like, he thought.

By the time he picked up the chalk, parts of the mob had reached the shops around his. The sound was deafening. Each footfall was a hammer, causing a disfiguring of words in his head, their twisting and crumbling, to reform into something he knew only by habit, not with heart. When he stood, he felt a hand on his collar and a sudden wrench, threatening to spill out his guts, holding his bones in a death trap.

The chalk slipped out of his fingers and fell, wriggling through a gap into the sewage slit and disappearing. Like words, like tongues and the way they curled to say 'azhagu'. How could he explain it to them? That the 'zh' was not the 'zh' of 'rag', but it was the 'zh' of 'rain', like the Americans say it when they are drunk, or how the Tamils say it naturally, the 'r' rising out from the nethers of the throat, laced with honey and cinnamon, their mutations shed like cocoons to burst out into butterflies. Beauty. That was what azhagu meant. Beauty, and it had to be spoken that way, or else it would sound really ugly.

He smelled the Hindi before he heard it bellowed into his ears.

The men handling him lifted him up and rammed him against the shutter. A ringing in the back of his skull, elbows folding against the metallic resistance of the shutter. What language did blood speak?

A punch into his gut. The air rushed out of his mouth, his eyes bulged like potatoes. How could he have not foreseen this? Spending far too much time at the library, his mother would say, with that god of words, those curled-up motes of dust narrating ancient stories in their fanciful words.

"Do you understand this, Kota?" one of the men questioned the other, their eyes flitting towards the name board over the shop, at the sprawl of Tamil in white against a chestnut canvas. The color of books and old envelopes.

The other clicked his tongue. "Fucking Madrasi thinks he can talk whatever he wants."

Perumal closed his eyes, awaiting the next punch.

In that gasping moment, he heard the reluctance of his assaulters and their stinking breath on his face.

When he opened his eyes, he smelled rain. The hands holding him had not weakened, and yet Perumal felt a strange companion in the water from the skies. The slow trickle of drops from the slope of his shop's roof, pattering on his head, rolling down his cheek and over his nose, foraying into his mouth.

It steadily rose, falling on the street, a hazy curtain of needled water, bouncing over the puddles and spraying on to the mob's tunics; onto Perumal's own jaded cottons as his mind strayed from his struggle to break himself free of the henchmen's grip.

Saaral. The gentle, secondary drizzle from rain, that seaspray bleaching his face as he imagined standing on the prow of a galley on rocky waters, that – no, that was not right. Something was missing. A flavor, perhaps, or perhaps 'gentle' was not the right word. If he had to impress the god of words, or worse, make him endure, he would have to find a way to communicate beside what was being forbidden. And yet this was saaral.

Saaral. As he breathed the word out, the hands clasping his shirt loosened. The two men exchanged glances before their eyes veered to the skies.

What had begun as a drizzle intensified in a matter of seconds into a downpour. The skies cracked, breathing thunder. Raindrops like pincers pierced the mob and began to flood the street.

The mob paused in their rancor, and the minister on the jeep called to his followers to abandon whatever it was they were doing and rush to him. Their hate could wait. This was no time to begrudge the rain.

Perumal felt himself slump against the shutter, drenched, hair falling over his forehead, a saltiness in his mouth. The hundreds who had streamed into the street began to run the opposite way, kerchiefs over their heads, stumbling and tripping over each other, trailing the fleeing jeep, seeking shelter.

Saaral. The more Perumal whispered it, lying against the shutter of his shop, the fiercer fell the torrent. The fleeing mob was a blur, moving shades of black under a canvas of gray. He was now afraid to utter 'mazhai', the word for rain itself. It lingered on his lips like an apology, a change of heart, a feeling from the bottommost pit of his heart. He wanted to experiment, but he looked around and saw nothing but the abandoned memory of his home. Beside him, still clad in the veil of her saree, the chemist hunched with her mouth open, her hand outstretched at the razing deluge.

"What is this?" she uttered in disbelief as water pattered over her palm. "It's April!"

Perumal shrugged, brushed the water off his eyes and stood. The jeep, the man upon it and the henchmen had left. The rain drowned their sounds, covering up their muddy tracks and swallowing the flags and stones they had abandoned on the road.

Perumal turned towards the chemist. "Sorry about the chalk. I lost it."

"Look," she said. "Once the rain stops, it's best you change the name, yes? They will come back. They are going from state to state, town to town, lane to lane until they get what they want."

Perumal had long since tried to piece together what the mob, and the ministers whipping them, wanted. If he had thought they would stop with one religion, he was grossly mistaken. Religion had only been the beginning. There was a deeper, more intrinsic, disagreement with diversity.

He wished to return home, but the bookstore was holding him back. Every incident, every incitement and flare sent up into the skies weakened the god of words, lying beneath the shop, clinging to untranslated manuscripts and stories abandoned in the last decades. It was Perumal's duty, as it had been of his father and mother and their ancestors before, to placate the god of words, to feed him with plurality until he calmed and did not rain dust on their faces. Today was no different from widening that rift between Perumal and his work.

With 'saaral' on his lips he dashed back inside, down the spindly stairs to that dark chamber where the god of words lay in his rattled breathing, his body no more than decomposed paper in the shape of a sleeping corpse. Perumal was careful not to disturb the construction and sat beside the god, shivering.

He then sang a song in ancient Tamil, each word pronounced like a spell, as though he were in the arms of Poonkuzhali, that brave boat woman in the epic *Ponniyin Selvan*, who had rode the stormy seas, rescued two princes and became queen.

Slowly, dust settled on Perumal's thighs and the god of words rumbled awake.

There was not much left in him now. Perumal suppressed his tears and blew some of the dust towards the carapace of torn paper.

"Ask me more questions."

The god of words breathed out in wrinkles and crumples. "I don't have any more."

"Gi-give me more words, then. Something. Anything."

The dust quaked, like it was undergoing a seizure. "You already have everything you need."

Perumal blinked. "I don't. What am I supposed to do?"

But the god of words was silent again. The dust settled on the floorboards, the haze melting into clarity. Barely a conversation's worth of life. He had once held a repository of endless songs and poems, tributes to fallen linguists and revolutionaries with placards that burned in eternal flame. Perumal had been witness to that since he was a child, burrowing beneath the bookstore with his father, who held a torch in his mouth and introduced him to the god of words. *Say hello*, he remembered his father's words. *Say hello, only in a way you have never said it before. Say it in a way that leaves no scope for goodbye.*

Perumal continued muttering 'saaral' under his breath, but it had to stop at some point. Give way to something more meaningful, more mundane. Even his thoughts lay blocked beneath a barricade of that one word, his guardian.

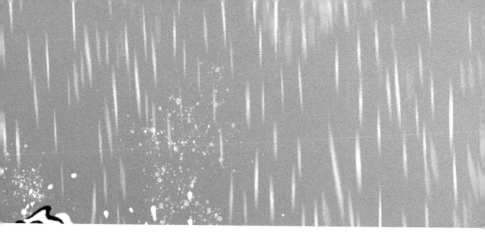

Slowly, he rose, re-arranged a few of the shelves and crates and climbed back to the bookstore. In darkness he sought a candle, and lit it up, and gazed at the shadows on the bindings. He walked to the farthest end, steeped in shadow, and, from beneath a pile of rotten leather, picked out the copy of *Ponniyin Selvan*. He flipped through the pages until he settled on an inscription of Poonkuzhali, leaning out of her boat's prow, a gaze of beauty and longing etched in those eyes that Perumal could never forget. His fingers grazed the words beneath the image, and they lingered there until Perumal was certain that he would be an idiot to not try.

Outside, the patter of rain mimicked his beating heart. Once he placed the book back under the stack, he ambled over to the shutter and undid the holds. The screws creaked and the metalwork groaned. When he peered out, the fragrance of rain hit him, with splashes of saaral.

Silence. Water flowing down the road, light brown and marsh-like in appearance, with a flotsam of newspapers, sandals and stools. Madhu uncle's little boy stretched one foot ahead from the provision store opposite, teasing the flow, wrapping loose bits of tissues around his toes. Before Perumal could holler at him, Madhu uncle slithered out of his house and, scooping his son in his arms, shot an apologetic look in Perumal's direction, and retreated to slam the door shut.

Warily, Perumal stopped muttering saaral.

The rain did not abate at once, but gradually lessened to a steady drizzle, allowing the water to seep through the edges of the concrete, or through the slits on the manhole covers. The chemist returned with an umbrella, a deep frown on her face as she regarded Perumal through thick-rimmed glasses.

When she spoke, she spoke in Hindi, broken and accented, punctured with longing. "You're a big fool, Perumal."

"I'm not going to answer you in their language, you know that," he retorted. "Not this way. This is what they want."

"And they will get it, pulla. It's the only language they know, and if you can't answer them in a way they understand, they will believe you are against them." She paused, pulling her face back an inch and wiping her glasses with a tissue. "You know, your mother always told me to watch out for your stupidity."

"I'd rather be whipped a fool than bow in shame, auntie. Please go back inside, now. I'll come to you later for some band-aid and soframycin."

The chemist scoffed, hunched her shoulders and retreated within her shop. A clack of metal told Perumal that she had locked herself in.

He took a deep breath and scanned the road once again. When the silence descended on him fully, he closed his eyes and invaded the depths of this thoughts.

All he heard at first was a horn. The sound of a roaring engine. And then a clamor of footsteps. So much for words on a name board, he thought, and smiled to himself.

Quietly, he uttered 'arumbu'. The word for a bud that was not yet a bud but had begun to sprout nonetheless. The translation was stunted, the infancy of the bud barely comprehensible unless he wove through the mesh of the original tongue and scooped it in its entirety. The echo of it swam through the mud water to the beginning of the street where it sunk to the tarmac, cobbled by waste and pebbles. By the time the jeep could enter, the bud that had not yet been a bud had blossomed into a tree, branches shooting sideways, cordoning the path entirely. One of the roots must have spiraled underneath the jeep, for the motor whizzed and droned, caught in the tangles of the strange wood and earth.

Heart galloping in his chest, Perumal felt his breath leave him. He stepped out of the threshold of his shop and planted his feet into the puddle. One step and then another until he stood in the center of the street, knee-deep in water, facing the impaled jeep. The minister screamed orders to his henchmen, most of whom had frozen at the sight of the sudden creation in front of their eyes.

The moment slid away like weak resistance. The ones on the jeep got down and struck to hacking at the branches with scythes and billhooks. The ones who got through were the most enraged, eyes only for Perumal, who by then had lost some of his nerve and took a step back to gauge the situation.

'Tulir', he whispered apprehensively, and the branches shook to unleash a storm of leaves. Tulir, which was a baby leaf, yet more than that. It was coddled with tenderness and freshness, taunted by a delicate touch and the smell of fresh dew and monsoon mornings that evoked the word on Perumal's lips in a rush of forested wetness. The leaves were as large as banyan's, wrapping the henchmen like wet curtains until every step of theirs was a stumble, down to the taste of mud and waste.

The ones wading towards him through the knee-deep puddle held knives and pistols. Perumal could now feel the god of words inside his head, his breath in his own, tongue stitching with his, the knots binding them, memory flooding back in treacherous waves that threatened to lap over his insides and stream out in a babble of forgotten words.

Palaar. The henchman who had raised the gun in Perumal's direction felt the slap on his cheek before he could pull the trigger. He crashed into the water, gun and all, and did not rise again. Palaar was not the slap itself; it was the anger, the drive and the ferocity behind it. It was the admonishment of a wrong act, the vengeance seethed in the skin running over the palm. Perumal dug into the sinews of his arms, into his clenched fists as he whispered the word each time. It had to be a whisper. They did not deserve the tenacity of his voice, only the underlying injustice it was subjected to.

Palaar. Palaar. Palaar.

The whisper carried through the waters in faint ripples.

Every henchman that remained on this side of the monstrous tree was sinking into the waters, blade-held hand clutching the cheeks, pain seared into the flesh.

And although Perumal did not laugh, the god of words did, working Perumal's mouth into a jubilant release of joy.

Perumal watched with every breath that passed out of his body as the jeep, the minister on it, and his loyal henchmen scrambled to escape. He glanced at the headboard, at the name in Tamil that had lured the minister and his hunters by the stink of its curves and strangeness.

By the time they were gone, Perumal had sunk to his knees, water floating around his belly, a newspaper poking his rib, flashing a soaked headline in Hindi he did not bother to understand.

'Mazhai', he whispered at last, and the rain fell, harsher than ever on the street, dragging with it the chalk boards and the saffron-painted benches in its flood. The god of words finally calmed, folding himself like a crumpled piece of parchment, his endurance dragging him through another day.

Fighting his tears, Perumal craned his neck up to the skies with his eyes closed, rain piercing his face, the image of Poonkuzhali shimmering in his mind as she rowed the boat through the storm, towards home.

Prashanth is a financial consultant who spends his evenings buried in fantasy tomes or maps of his own making. His works have appeared, or recently been selected to appear, in *Beneath Ceaseless Skies* and *AHF magazine*. He lives in Bangalore, India, with his wife and Kittu the cat.

ACADEMIA LUNARE

TIES THAT BIND:
LOVE IN FANTASY AND SCIENCE FICTION

EDITED BY FRANCESCA T BARBINI

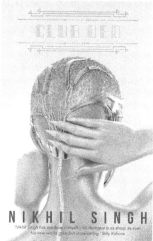

CLUB DED

NIKHIL SINGH

'Nikhil Singh has outdone himself - his dialogue is as sharp as ever, his new world grim but intoxicating.' Billy Kahora

Uncanny Bodies

Edited by Pippa Goldschmidt,
Gill Haddow and Fadhila Mazanderani

Science Fiction, Fantasy & Dark Fantasy in Fiction and Academia.

Luna Press PUBLISHING

Academia Lunare LUNA PRESS PUBLISHING

Scottish Independent Press
Est. 2015

www.lunapresspublishing.com

THE
PLEASURE
OF
DROWNING
JEAN BURLESK

THE EMERALD TREE
NINA ORAM

BOOK II OF THE CARROWKEEL SERIES

The Satanic
in Science Fiction
and Fantasy

A J DALTON

BLOODBUSTERS
FRANCESCO VERSO

TRANSLATED BY SALLY McCORRY

THE COLOUR OF
MADNESS

PAUL KANE

WHERE THE
OCEAN MEETS
THE SKY

Barbara Stevenson

SONS OF
STORM
FRANCESCA NOTO

**MACH
INER
IES OF
MERCY**

TIM MAJOR

Sakahlu Homeland

D.A. Xiaolin Spires

We only see him in this one confined space. In some other realm – we know it's another realm since the light is different there: more diffused, softer – he plays a rare instrument. The *sakahlu*, a banned thing. But this one isn't made of the typical wood and silk. It's one made of dissident bones. *These are the exact bones from those who are said to have simply disappeared,* cultivated from The Fulcrum's DNA Bank of the Deceased.

He stole into it, they say. No one knows how he did it.

The Bank is sealed in multiple layers of safe images that vary at any given moment: three strands of onyx hair blowing in the wind, the way the skin of pomegranate shines when newly applied with wax, the laces of hovershoes, pink neons projected from holographic traffic paws. I found these examples of security imagecodes when I looked it up. Of course these images are no longer in use since they've been rendered to the public by the so-called (as proclaimed by The Fulcrum) "radicals," the hosts who ran the HTW (How-Things-Work) holocast, in their episode about security tech. They disappeared soon afterward, too.

The technology hasn't changed that much since. The images that are currently in use are repeated in certain ways and interlaced, such thick continuous overlays that there is no way he could penetrate them all.

And, yet, *he* has.

His instrument, as it appears covertly on underground screens scattered throughout the city: two round-ish bones at the end separated by a bridge of strings, like a vamped-up dumb-bell. A visual now considered so contraband that The Fulcrum will confiscate anything that looks like it: barbell eyebrow rings, balled coat hooks, fidget yo-yos.

I'm sharing a protein pot stew with Yubahs and Timmahs. Yubahs slaps my hand, telling me to stop picking out the twisted protein bow ties. They're the most edible things in there. He says, poking at the pot, "These round-ish bones are just a construction, without any deep meaning."

I stab two more bow ties from the stew and pop them in my mouth. They taste like static with a subdued malty flavor – not great at all – but at least the texture isn't bad. Yubahs slaps me in the back with a pretend pat and the bow tie goes down the wrong way.

"There are no bones," I say, coughing. "Just hybromeat."

Yubahs rolls his eyes. "Kebel dummy. We're talking about Kebel and his *sakahlu*. You know, ding-a-ling?" He pretends to strum.

"Not talking about the protein pot," he hisses, miming bringing a spoon to his mouth and X-ing it out.

"Not everything is about food," Timmahs says. He shoves hot stew into his mouth, chewing on a particularly tough nugget. "Yubahs is wrong. The body of his instrument is not just some construction. The round ends have meaning; they're not crafted, they've been reappropriated. What does Yubahs know anyway?"

Everyone picks on Yubahs. He's not the youngest nor the scrawniest – I take the cake for both those attributes. But, he's prone to being morose, which in our sibling-value system, is a far worse trait.

Yubahs frowns, as if on cue, kicking the pot. Stew spills and he cleans it up, knowing Ma could walk in at any moment.

Timmahs draws a picture in the air with his metal chopsticks. "His *sakahlu*. They're two pelvic bones, overt symbols of sexuality," Timmahs continues, smirking. He swallows, his fingers dropping his chopsticks. He's the only one who bothers with the utensil; we prefer eating with our hands. Timmahs pretends to pluck an invisible instrument. "...and Kebel's fingers brush against the negative space in the middle where the strings lie – a kind of subversive act."

He stops, taking a hold of the audience around him, letting the image sink in. We snort, stomping our feet. Timmahs gives his imaginary instrument another strum. His eyes dart, knowing that such lascivious talk will certainly have him sent to the sensory-deprivation zone of charged particles besides the linen closet, or the "the flat tickle" as we call it once the switch is on, the mother of all time-outs. I look around – no, Ma's not here.

Timmahs presents the instrument and by the way he traces its fictitious outlines, I can almost see it, the two mounds bolted together by the plane that stretches across. I wonder if the twin bodies of the instrument really are reproduced pelvic bones. I imagine them forming together, not layer by layer as the old reproductions, but in more efficient piece-able chunks, jigsaw pieces fitting, interlocking and growing into each other, engineered from blueprints gleaned from the DNA bank.

We sit back, extend our legs, massage our arms. From the harmonic sighs I know my brothers are thinking about Kebel's instrument. The plaintive sounds of its twin bodies tinkle in my ears.

I pick out the last of the protein bits from my teeth, lick my gums and suck on a remaining piece of star anise. I let the sweet bitterness melt into my tongue as I consider the string instrument's form. It's an instrument that shouldn't exist. It defies logic, a fretboard between these two bony "pelvic" ends, with strings made of dissident guts, so at least they say. The entirety of it is made of cobbled parts reproduced through stolen genes. These were the genes of heroes, martyrs – our people – those who were tortured, eviscerated before being copied onto files and stowed away in the Great Warehouses. Journalists, prominent politicians, athletes.

There are things we don't say. They are brought forth into the world by the disturbance of our communal breaths in the air, in our pauses. I don't mention Lika and Dovahla, our missing twin sisters. They are a stunning pair with fast feet whose *guhlap* skills were unparalleled. They would kick the duo-hoverballs – so much like the *sakahlu* in shape – a pair of soccer balls connected by string propelled by their feet in such high arcs that when the balls wrapped around the goalposts, it was almost as if they were compelled by forces from outside this plane.

On their 18th birthdays, before they disappeared, we painted the likeness of their faces onto *guhlap* ball-decorated cakes, their edible smiles looking back at us. Their (actual) expressions that day when they saw the cake were one of the last I've seen of them that emanated such pure joy – smiles that continue to haunt me.

After that, their gameplay fumbled, their eyes displayed a nervous gleam and they tripped over each other often. No longer working as a pair, a concert of legs, but rather, four individual, autonomous and anxious feet. I wonder if they were purposely sabotaging their careers – and then, well, they disappeared. And let's not talk about how Ma took that, especially since Pa had been long gone – and we can't talk about that either.

We also don't mention our own musical talents, our disbanded quartet, not with Mava also missing, "sent away."

Kebel is the only one of our people who has returned to us, even if it's just through these holovids. If we interpret his messages correctly, the main government can't pinpoint him accurately but they've found the particulate traces of the bubble where he operates.

We are about to finish our meal and return to our labor – working the presses, delivering propaganda or "ground breaking news" (as it always seems more real coming from a person, so The Fulcrum tells us) and sketching designs for the next courtyard displays.

We are about to leave the comfort of the hearth when our coasters on the table start to shine. That is the first warning. Our coasters, misshapen and worn, aren't fully tech-compatible. But, they have enough rigged into them to get a whiff of the transmission and at least begin to pulsate. We hide them away.

Once they're concealed, we run to the bars. We know which ones are amenable to his cause. We know which ones carry the diode coasters and menu sheets, where they whisk away the unsympathetics and his images for an instance grace these everyday items, rendered into pixelated momentary Kebel-branded bric-a-brac. I can't wait to get there. My legs convert this enthusiasm into a full-on sprint. Even so, I can barely keep up with my brothers.

My chest heaves as I pass billboards. It's never the billboards. We never see his face prominently displayed. It's always in the secluded, mundane spots.

I trip, my mouth hitting a hoverguard's scanning apparatus. They must also have sensed that the time is nigh. The uniformed hoverguard is about to scan my face and I lick blood, an acrid taste smeared on my lips. Timmahs pulls me up, sprays and wipes down the drops of blood on the ground with an illicit chromosomal-bleach travel pack. He tucks the rag and spray away back into his back pocket. With the swiftness of an experienced older brother, he covers my eyes with his hands, just as he pulls his neck in and his head down. We shuffle away quickly, taking a back route.

I look back for a second. The hoverguard follows us but then turns around as it zeroes in on someone else. Timmahs pulls my arm. I pull his arm back. "C'mon," he says. As we hurry away, I don't hear the ping that tells me they finish the scan. Good.

As I enter the bar, the Myriad Thirsts, there's a commotion then a hush as the doors close behind. They enter a pattern of fingerprint IDs. It's a blur, like a pianist playing an intricate melody. The lock clicks shut in response.

The lights are dimmed. It's already started. The stripes of The Fulcrum's banner on the flexiflags are giving way to a staticky blur.

The servers pass out the "heavenly brew," a mix of mostly beer and a house-distilled liquor, the bootleg concoction topped with a familiar stick. The banned barbell stirrer. I pick up the rounded top, like a tiny scepter. So smooth in my fingers, so ergonomic, there's almost a power to it in its sleek precision, and I begin to whirl the drink, soaking in the eye-stinging fumes. My brothers do the same, Yubahs swirling with such rigor that he spills his heavenly brew in the process. The server comes over and tries to wipe it up, but I beat him to it. I throw a gleaming smile at Yubahs and he smiles back. He's just as excited as me.

The server, with his work taken from him, decides instead to pass out the coasters. We don't pull the drinks onto them. No, we peer into them like crystal balls, our eyes probing for a tomorrow better than today. We've been waiting for this and there's a palpable hush that spreads across the bar.

On the coasters, the blocky font of the bar's signature logo recedes and we see the downturned lips of Kebel. We see his hair getting greyer, but his energy is still there. He commands the presence of his limited space, that backdrop of grassland that we can never tell if it's real or a projection. And once he has our souls affixed to him – it always seems that he knows we're attuned – he begins to play.

We sit back and mutter along with him. None of us, not my brothers, not the many men and women in the room, busy tired homemakers, the working stiff, are ready to croon boldly aloud yet. We rock back and forth, holding ourselves, singing quietly.

Every day at any given time, usually but not always on the hour, his face appears in clandestine screens in certain establishments. Small private flexiflags that wave with patriotic dignity convert to a picture of subversion. There was once a time you could see his face on large flexiflags alongside the highway, but The Fulcrum picked it up in no time and they have long since taken down the flags, and replaced them with the hack-proof analog analogs. Pre-flexiflag. Flappy, fabric things that no longer convert to moving images. But, even as they've removed the capability of his face to be plastered there, still, his presence seeps in in other ways.

The gruff voices of disaffected laborers surround me in a quiet euphony. Tired of the demands of the all-encompassing Fulcrum, they hum and sing quietly of grasslands and faraway geographical beauties.

I can't help but strum in the air as I watch the hypnotic, precise movements of Kebel's slender fingers. These screen coasters are cheap ones, and he is blurred and the writing behind him is barely legible. Our brothers learned how to read it because of our shared musical background, but not everyone knows. The writing behind Kebel says something to the likes of: "Follow the rays of light from the sun, where it illuminates the right and casts shadows on the wrong. See how each blade of grass absorbs such light or withers."

Not everyone knows what the words behind him say. Our language is diminishing so much so it is mostly oral, and now more creole than unitary, mixed in with common Fulcra. But it is enough that he is there, singing our forgotten words. Words that are echoed back to him in whispers in houses.

The Myriad Thirsts, this pub, is one of the most sympathetic to our people. It's run by our people. Some other pubs in The Fulcrum removed Kebel, threw out these coasters – even pubs run by some prominent community leaders. They told dissidents to go away and stop planting propaganda in their establishments.

Discard divers salvaged the coasters before The Fulcrum recombinated them. It's not really about where loyalties lie, but more about playing it safe. It's not that these pubs are unsympathetic, per se, but they fear the closure by state more than they are willing to risk listening to his words. But the Myriad Thirsts knows better. They embrace his presence and know that his seeping voice is good for business. It's good for their own sense of being. It's why we gather here more than anywhere else.

We nod along and tap our feet as his deep voice takes on a sonic boom, his charged notes inflected with a twang that carries a folksy reverberation, tugging at the soul of every one of us.

I get up and dance. So do others. We are the *Megum* people, our peppy feet seem to say. They tried to indoctrinate us, but here it is – that folk, that bucolic longing that rings through our bodies. It's romantic, it's idyllic – we know it's a pipe dream and it crashes hard into our being as we move. Some of our community members sit there, shaking, holding drinks, sipping, some with tears streaming while pretending not to cry all at the same time. By this time I am laughing, crying and my brothers are laughing with me.

He shouldn't exist. But he does.

Behind Kebel, in his projection through the coaster, his regeneration machine lights up. It makes a warm-up sound, a hum that sits pitch-wise just above Kebel's own tremoloing tenor and below the urgent strum, disconsolate and pleading at once.

The whispers say The Fulcrum send a constant barrage of attempts to transport dangerous things into his sanctified domain, but Kebel's superior security system wipes those away. Recently, he's had his regeneration machine moved to the top of his bubble.

The pessimists say he has not updated his security. They call it a lack of strategy. But some say it is a political move, so every so often, black tea or some other fluid appears from the regenerator, spilling into his place. He purposely has his regeneration machine located at top of his domain so it spills down into his room. We know from these incidents that there is a kind of gravity there and we have debates on where it might be out there in the universe and how the physics work.

When the liquid does fall, it sprinkles onto the edges of his robe and sprays into some areas of the room, sometimes hitting his instrument, but most of it splashes over the intelliboard behind him. The message on the board changes with the interaction. Sometimes it interacts with the liquid and transforms into a riddle: "Why do the stars twinkle?... Because they blink for a moment of darkness that hides the truth."

This time it says: "Ball and chains lose their shackles, becoming a tool that tackles."

I can't help but chuckle every time. I sit back down, cover my mouth, catch my breath. It seems funny, all these prosaic things spilling into his space throughout his pronouncements: tea, squid ink, pomegranate juice, salad dressing, even protein stew. A buffet of hurled insults rendered into liquid canvases.

"There The Fulcrum goes again, trying to overload his system," says Yubahs, but we shush him as he's taking us out of the sanctified moment. Kebel's starting a new song. But, what Yubahs says is right, The Fulcrum tries to send him anything and everything, shooting out recombination patterns until one, that we're sure Kebel's security algorithm vets, goes through. The whole performance is, in a way, designed by Kebel, as Timmahs once said. These liquids sent by The Fulcrum trickle past the words Kebel has scrawled in *peahtty ink* and reveal the underlayer,

only visible through the interaction with the traces of the recombination particles that the regeneration machine emits.

It's genius, I think, as I continue to mutter along to his songs.

Another splash from the regeneration machine. From within the image of the coasters, the projected Kebel wipes it off the twin body of his *sakahlu* with his sleeve, tracing up the reverberating strings. And we see the identifying neon message of the regenerator that it's soy sauce before the liquid trickles onto the intelliboard. And it's like The Fulcrum doesn't learn that its tactics are being reappropriated for indoctrination against its own High Institution.

Here spells another proverb about space, that propels Kebel's agenda and philosophy. Some say he is out there, orbiting, watching down on us, stuck in his own prison but free in a sense. A hum goes around as the older laborers and homemakers translate the message to the younger generation.

I take out a hidden journal and catalog his message, noting the lyrics, writing in a script that is much censured and hidden away. I skim through the previous songs as Kebel takes a break, sipping nectar.

I skim my scattered pages, my fingers tracing the curved script. He sings these longing songs of homeland, of a better time, of a future, of a people united. They are not overtly political, in the way many things are not overtly political. About separation. About the stars that separate them. About having not seen the sea. And recently – about seeing the volcano, its inviting maw full of hot breath.

He clears his throat and puts down the mug of nectar. *Departure is coming*, he says with wet lips, and blinks. Then he sings a nasal one-note tune, holding out the high-pitched note. It persists. He speaks while holding this tune out – a wonder of control of his vocal cords – about the Milky Way that is supposed to carry us, deliver us to our better worlds. He's never done this before.

I stop writing and stare into the coaster. His ability to overtone chant, considered an extinct art form, bowls me over. Then I look at my brothers. Their faces are backlit with the brightness of Kebel's greying beard and hair. We all bristle. I see his image repeated, staring hard at us, holding out this tune as if he doesn't need to breathe. I marvel at this meme-like face smattered all over tables of spilled alcoholic concoctions in this dark hideout.

The streaks of soy sauce interacting with the intelliboard, congealing behind him, look eerily like the Milky Way, that beautiful cosmic river whose one symbolic heft is an escape route to redemption.

The Fulcrum destroyed all ships from the last escape attempt twenty years ago. It was a small group, only a fraction of our community. But, The Fulcrum met a tiny flame with an army of extinguishers. They tore down the tourist industry, sacrificing an economy with so much potential for their need for control. They took over the sector – reprogramming destination coordinates to only acceptable colonies. There is a long wait to travel anywhere since then, and those in our community are flat-out rejected from leaving. The Fulcrum built VR machines, instead, that have limited settings. *You want to travel?* is their sneer. *Sure, then travel with your mind.*

I've shuffled past these pages that I've written about the tourism scuffle. I flip past sketched images of Kebel in my journal. I'm taking a catalog of it all, matching his face to the one I see that is starting to fade from the coasters. The people are waking from their trance, this engagement with a spiritual leader we have long missed.

Is he just a projection of a disaffected mass? Some people say he is not real, that there are operatives in the government that have gone rogue and they have created him. That they imbued him with their own desires and fears, creating this figure haunted with a mix of shackles and freedom. People say that it is a projected sense of that cry for help, embodied into this likeness of a man.

In his voice is something that decries falsehood. He is real. My brothers begin to chat, rehashing old debates.

People say they knew him. That he existed. The older generation said that when they were young their parents had access to land and roamed. They said they saw him, touched his instrument, touched those calloused fingers and his long woolen coat.

They say he writes forwards and backwards, like the way his instrument is designed, ball to ball, no top no bottom, no front no end. He writes starting from the middle of a sentence and working in both directions. The words are sometimes left to right, sometimes right to left, but the meaning is clear. They are like the messages on the intelliboard behind him, as I say, contributing to my brothers' debates. In our script, we do not differentiate which direction to write and his messages, sometimes looping left and sometimes right, often reflect that ambiguity.

I inscribe the update to today's message, our voices now subdued as the pub unlocks its doors.

We leave.

The next time our coasters blink, it's a labor hour, but close enough to a break that it's safe to depart from our duties. I fetch my brothers and we steal away to a tiny outlet in the market.

In his song, Kebel tells us to wait for the days for the maternal volcano's maw to open wide and swallow us up. Once The Fulcrum's black vinegar is spilt, we see the intelliboard message is not to be afraid of the lava, for it doesn't burn. Wait for the river of magma which will take us far away. It will morph and bubble, because it is effervescent, transformative, but it will not scald. Kebel continues to sing, his voice uplifting, our souls quenched.

I don't know how many of us he has on the ground. All I do is tuck the coasters into specified locations that I find in stacks behind the bushes. It has always been my role. My brothers don't know about my activities but they must suspect. And I suspect they have their own roles. But to talk about them is to jeopardize all of us. Kebel has a catalog of dissidents.

I am at the bushes about to gather coasters, one hot sticky day, when I see their flat sides flashing. I panic and grab them, throwing them into my bag. As I run to the Myriad Thirsts, my heart beats loudly, feeling like it's shooting out of my chest. A prick in my spine jabs, telling me something is altogether different. Transformative. His face appears on all the screens. Not just the small flexiflags from sympathetic storefronts, but from billboards of official The Fulcrum buildings.

There he is, his magnificent greying beard, his downturned mouth, expressing not really disdain, but a kind of removal from the present.

I run along, knowing that in my bag there are stacks of him with his face glowing. I have to scatter these coasters quick. I've never had them glow on me before as I was handling them in my distribution role.

I sneak quite a few under the doorsteps of a few places, quick to dart and avoid cameras.

I retreat to the Myriad Thirsts.

It's exceptionally hot and there is a squall of terrible heat rain, one we have not experienced in decades. It is mixed with an atmospheric turbulence from The Load out west. An imbalance in the forces so that The Effort is no longer in harmony with The Load. The Load comes rolling in with heat and dust, not a tumble our way yet, but a slow progression. It mixes in the air and comes down in inky splashes, reminding me of the descriptions of the early skies when the first ships were forged to bring our people here.

The rain shifts from warm to burning hot. The ground is steaming.

There are more of us coming. We take cover in the Myriad Thirsts. I hand out cold-bearing blankets that have been stocked in the storeroom, presumably by those dissidents who have roles privy to seeing this coming. Our attention is to the outside; the owner has left the autoblinds open, for the first time during Kebel's projection.

I stand by the door, pressing the icy blanket to another community friend. The rain outside collects and pools together, with oily iridescence.

"Strange," he says, staring outside, grabbing the blanket and putting his face into it. "Ah, nice and cool," he says.

I give him a pat on the back.

The collected raindrops form statues and exhibit a luminousness to them, the twinkle of stars. These statues rise up towards the ethereal stretch of the Milky Way.

I realize: they are pointing towards a path.

We gasp in collective recognition. They are ships.

I know I am in the Myriad Thirsts. But, from Kebel's voice and the view of these statue-ships, I am already transported.

"Another blanket, please," says a woman with piercing eyes, wearing a scarf.

"Here," I mumble, arm outstretched. I see the crows feet around her eyes as she delivers a smile. She takes it, but my focus wanders. I barely notice that she is complaining about how icy the blanket is.

When these city-wide images of Kebel sing, it's like the land is opening up itself. It shakes The Fulcrum, rattling the pith – the very pivot base of our once-stable see-saw. The earth teeters. Blankets fall out of my arms. I hear his voice coming from the ground and feel it in my bones.

A newfound freshness washes over me.

There we can roam and there are no cameras. There we have work, but no mandated labor, no suppression, only the gentle guiding of wind that brings the grass to rustle and wave in capricious greetings.

We wait for all the squalls to stop so we may emerge. I pluck out of my bag a few items: my journal, a satchel full of instant protein pot and a handful of coasters. I count my things, return them to the bag and stuff in a cold-bearing blanket. I don't know if it matters anymore; if the tech will work where we are heading. If the coasters will illuminate, if the blankets will hold the frigid. In my hair, I hide a number of barbell pins with embedded decoding tech. If they become analog, then so be it.

Some say it is a trick, that the path will lead to destruction, that we will all be put into bubbles just like him. That we will tumble off this see-saw of life and end up in the abyss. That he is trapped and it is a governmental ploy. It is a means for The Fulcrum to eradicate us.

But, for those who believe, and we cannot help but believe, that's all we have left. We get up and our bones ache for our lost brethren and for our dissipating culture. We feel as if our particles do not spin anymore, are not governed by the same properties that govern the rest of the universe, that we are barely alive here. When it is time, we will trickle out and tread our way to these forged ships.

I imagine The Fulcrum Forces will be held back. I know they will not be able to approach us even as they march. Our brittle but determined pelvic bones will move to a beat together. Whatever it is that contains Kebel in his safe playing room, wherever it may be, at once a liberation, at once a jail, at once "somewhere out there," these military forces too will be held behind, trapped in the same substance that holds Kebel safe.

I see this image I hold in me unravel before my eyes. It feels as real to me as Kebel himself. I don't know if this image is prophetic, lucky or if this is just exigent times exciting my senses. Yet, everything unfolds as it should. We are marching. We move our tense pelvises, dancing in a way. My visions come to being.

The Fulcrum Forces are held back by a compulsion outside their control.

As I see my brothers marching, almost too apprehensive to cheer next to me, yet with a determined smile plastered on their faces, I wonder, is it an indication that it is truly redemption we go to? Or is it only The Fulcrum who have access to these invisible borders, that are holding the borders up, protecting themselves from the volcanic flame that might engulf us? Perhaps keeping them safe from The Load that will roll over and crush us all?

The sound of bones tinkle. Little finger bones. Bones of instrument players. Clicky-clacks of chattering teeth. Vocalists. There are little barbell bones on strings being passed around by our brethren. We hang them off our arms, tie them to our legs, braid them to our hair as we march. The spaceships approach, forged from falling liquids and looking impossibly tall.

The sound of the tinkling of these DNA replicated bones of our past dissidents fills the air. The conspiring images of Kebel symphonize as they sing of a place where the flesh will grow back in places it has desiccated. Where fat will grow in and bounce where it no longer lies. It is a very unusual song for him to sing, all focused on the body, about rejuvenation. Not landscapes, not steppes, but our very flesh.

To the ships, we sing.

We climb in. It's surprisingly cool. As cool as the shade, away from the sun. The refrain of song hits me. It's about rays of light and living in the shadows.

The pods are almost filled now.

The spaceships awaken. The sachets of instant protein pot powder in my bag rattle like percussive shakers, adding a soft rhythm to the growing voices who are singing Kebel's song. We remember the sounds, these words that have been alienated from us. We try to match his deep voice.

We take off, in multiple directions. People say it is to confuse The Fulcrum, so they won't come after us.

Are we the unsavory elements being ejected into the void? That is the pessimist view whispered by some of the folks who are too afraid to hope, but yet, too timid to stay behind. They choose the possibility of ejection to persecution.

The optimist view sees us already joining him. Entering the space where Kebel sits and plays the *sakahlu*, strumming with instruments of our own, producing our own calluses to preserve our history. His bubble growing until it covers a grand space. The boundaries recede and not only are there steppes, but also sinewy houses, evanescent strings holding them up and barbell door handles that don't represent any abstract Load and Effort held together by a Fulcrum, but instead twin balls of balance that pervade our culture. Seemingly impossible, these houses waver and tremble at each pluck and shiver at each strum.

This is what I see, what appears in my head: a sweeping vista of hope.

And I can smell it already. From each house, comes the aroma of protein pot stew, not just made of generic computative protein, not these instant sachets, not reduced to the algorithms of The Fulcrum to keep us laborers alive, but from something much more, rich and pungent, emanating of the soils of our land.

D.A. Xiaolin Spires steps into portals and reappears in Hawai'i, NY, Asia and elsewhere, with her keyboard appendage attached.
Her work appears in *Clarkesworld, Analog, Nature, Terraform, Fireside, StarShipSofa, Andromeda Spaceways (Year's Best)*, and also in anthologies such as *Future Visions, Broad Knowledge and Deep Signal*.
Find her on @spireswriter or daxiaolinspires.wordpress.com.

The Digital Man

Asith Pallemulla

Mrs Swanson walked home as inconspicuously as she could manage. Of course, the black briefcase she carried made it nearly impossible to be entirely anonymous. The lousy things, she thought. No one in their right mind still used them, and yet, that corporation insisted on them even though the thing inside the briefcase was so miniscule that it could have fitted in her pocket. She had considered opening it and taking out the package, leaving the case behind, but felt that doing this might draw attention to herself, or damage the thing inside, so she simply headed home as fast as she could.

It wouldn't be too difficult, she lived quite near the corporation. Not that it had mattered to her before – she hadn't had to set foot in there before today. Mrs Swanson didn't work there, though she had been asked to, once – her programming skills were relatively well known in the industry – but of course, she declined. Not after what her husband had done. Fortunately, she'd had Cynthia inside the business who did. It hadn't been easy to get the package. Mrs Swanson had begged her friend

Art: Cat Hellisen

63

to give it to her. Cynthia had initially refused. This wasn't an item that should leave the corporation under any circumstances. Weeks of bartering and arguing had followed, until that was eventually replaced by outright blackmail. Mrs Swanson had eventually gotten what she'd wanted.

Her hand shook as she held it up to the glowing touch-security system on her door, so much so that she had to attempt it thrice before it allowed her inside her home. She didn't dawdle, and booted up her computer system the minute she got in, afterwards opening the suitcase, revealing a miniature, green, digital chip that looked far too delicate for what it contained.

Mrs Swanson slipped the microchip into her computer's scanning dock. It was simple enough, not unlike the USBs that had once been popular. She tingled with excitement, and perhaps a little fear, at what she was about to do.

The computer asked her whether she wished to run the program. She replied "Yes", a little more loudly than she needed to.

"Corporate Think-Tank; SWANSON," blared her computer, as it rendered the chip's program.

Mrs Swanson held her breath. The computer's announcement had triggered her sense of reality. It was finally happening. She had been fixated on this for months – there was no turning back. She was doing this.

The shape was beginning to forge itself on her computer screen, pixels fusing together, growing almost organically from something strangely embryonic into something more substantial. It was the shape of a man, in great detail, but more` importantly than that – the shape would be accompanied by the man's consciousness. The corporation's CEO's very essence was being drawn inside her computer. It would be a perfect copy, self-aware. It would quite literally be Mr Swanson himself.

It was almost sickening, what she was about to do. But frankly, she thought Mr Swanson had been entirely sickening too. Some people had called his idea sickening, once. The concept of pouring his consciousness into a computer program so that the corporation would never lose its CEO. His memories – his genius, as he called it – preserved for eternity. His being, ultimately simulated. Mrs Swanson would make the most of it.

The render was nearly complete. Her system was not nearly as powerful as the mainframe of the corporation – in fact, she had worried that she would not even be able to run the chip on her hardware – but it seemed to be functioning fine, albeit at a slower pace. Mrs Swanson would just have to keep her... methods, relatively simple.

The man in the computer was surrounded by darkness. He was the only thing in his realm of existence, for now. He opened his eyes. He seemed to have been ready with a hearty greeting, but faltered upon recognising Mrs Swanson as the user through the computer's camera: his window to the outside world.. His surprise showed Mr Swanson's memories were still perfectly intact.

"Hello dear," said Mrs Swanson. She began to realise that insanity had festered in her middle-aged brain, but she found that she did not care in the slightest.

"M-Margaret?" said the man. "How did you..."

"Oh, never you mind. Perhaps you should have invested in more security using the money you stole from me."

Mr Swanson's face changed. Perhaps, if he had been entirely human, it might have been different. He looked weary and wary – the expression of a man who had had this conversation far too many times, and did not look forward to repeating it in his technological eternity, but knew he had no choice. Fear began to inch across his pixellated face.

"Margaret, I know you think I wronged you –"

"You stole everything from me! It was MY idea."

"You wouldn't have known how to develop it properly! I turned your idea into a business, into a corporation."

"And that makes it alright?"

"Look, I offered you a job."

"Why would I work for a thief? You took everything we had and left me."

"You didn't want to use your idea properly! It would have been a waste. I only wanted to build a stable future for us."

"You mean for you."

"For us. You just refused to participate."

The man in the computer had lost his chance. Perhaps, deep down, there would have been a shred of forgiveness buried in Mrs Swanson's otherwise broken heart that could have been brought out by the right words. But Mr Swanson's words had been the same wrong words they'd always been, and Mrs Swanson was reminded of why she was doing this.

"Right," she said calmly. She rendered her holographic keyboard.

The digital man became visibly terrified. It seemed that he knew what was about to happen – he was about to meet a cruel God.

Mrs Swanson furiously typed into her keyboard with all the skill of a programmer and all the haste of a madwoman. The chip had rendered the man, but everything around the man? Well, that was her playground.

The first few lines of code she typed were simple enough: she flooded the scene. Tectonic amounts of water suddenly appeared on the screen, and the digital man found himself at the bottom of a digital ocean. Mr Swanson gasped and struggled, precious bubbles of air having already escaped from his mouth the second the water had appeared. He flailed his arms instinctively, looking for the surface, but of course, no end to this waterworld had been programmed.

Looking at the mortally terrified man who already seemed to be on the verge of suffocation in the great blue expanse, Mrs Swanson lost any remaining doubt. This was exactly what she'd wanted. The ocean had been a warning shot – she would no longer hesitate to use something worse.

It was true, of course, that Mr Swanson, being digital, would not be inherently capable of drowning. Not unless Mrs Swanson added her own code to the mix. But his consciousness, being an exact replica of his human brain, instincts and all, fully believed that he could. And that was the horror that Mrs Swanson enjoyed inflicting – the terror of being in mortal danger, only to survive and go through more. It would be, in her eyes, valid retribution.

Mr Swanson gave up. He had yielded himself to the thought of drowning as the deranged woman looked on. But he was not so lucky. Just as the water was about to flow into his lungs – or just as he thought this was about to happen – the keyboard flashed, and the ocean disappeared. Mrs Swanson was delighted with her timing.

Mr Swanson, now on all fours, coughed and spluttered, gasping for air. He was instantly dry, of course; the computer did not render any remnant of the water. But the terror lingered in his psyche. Mr Swanson was an intelligent man, and he understood what was happening, technically speaking, but logic couldn't overrule instinct. He looked up at Mrs Swanson, as if to beg, but said nothing.

Mrs Swanson began typing again. She would use whatever method came into her head.

She removed the digital floor and made the man fall from an unimaginable height, at speeds that would not have even been possible under normal gravity. It was the purest form of torture. Just as he feared slamming into a ground that never came, she saved him. He stood, fine – but traumatised.

The fear was now permanently stencilled in the man's eyes. Perhaps this was only because he was digital; perhaps it was just the extent of the terror. But it was there, and Mrs Swanson was satisfied.

With the joys of fear-infliction finished, she decided to move on to pain. It would be well-deserved pain.

As the man whimpered, she coated the floor in fire. The flames burned orange, as far as the computer could animate, which was too much for the digital man. To him, it was an infinite hell: to her, it was temporary satisfaction.

Mrs Swanson took care to define what the fires would do. She made them scorch his skin, burn into his limbs, boil his muscles into the wrong shape and make his central nervous system explode. But he would not die.

The man screamed the loudest he had screamed so far. Mrs Swanson lowered the volume, but not all the way. She wanted to hear the screams.

Mrs Swanson did not bother turning off the fire. She let the flames continue to burn as she typed in her next step. In the middle of the fire, she coded in digital blades, and began slicing away at the man's scorched flesh. At times, she stabbed. A normal man may not have been able to differentiate between all the intense pains at this stage, but the digital man's brain calculated them perfectly.

Mrs Swanson's creations were functioning better than she could have hoped for, and she wanted this pain to be her husband's penultimate memory. She immediately delved deeper into the digital man's own code. As he screamed, and cried, and tried to peel off his own blackened skin before the blades got to it, Mrs Swanson attacked his mind, ripping out vital areas and programming new areas to experience *absolute* agony when she felt the original areas were grossly lacking. Eventually, he fell silent, vanishing into the fires of Mrs Swanson's computer.

Mrs Swanson blinked. She had been immersed in the experience. Her computer whirred from the hard work it had done. She breathed a sigh of relief.

If you'd asked her she would have told you that it had been therapeutic, and she wouldn't have hesitated to recommend the experience. Was it murder? Perhaps. But the death of a digital man could never be final. While this chip had been protected so well that she would never be able to duplicate him on her own, she had no doubt that they would have another copy of Mr Swanson backed up somewhere. Another digital man. The same digital man. This one had gotten what he deserved. If only she could find another one...

Asith Pallemulla is an 18-year-old sixth-former who was born in Sri Lanka, and has lived there for most of his life (but dipped his toes into the UK for five years). He spends his free time jamming out on his guitar, reading, and more aptly, writing short fiction about weird, speculative, or borderline concerning narratives...

The Seven Day Ghost

Feng Gooi

My **wife and I** had set up an appointment at Attis Grief Service to resurrect her dead father. As I was sitting in the lush green office, the slogan kept running through my head: Their death is not your ending. My wife sat next to me; she bit her lip in anxiety.

Surrounding the sleek modern desk was a bed of soft grass and stalks of bright yellow flowers. They stretched enthusiastically upwards, reaching out to the sunlight pouring into the office. They probably symbolized rebirth or something.

"Their death is not your ending." The voice that said those words was calm and maternal yet crackling with emotion. With it came an undercurrent of hope and happiness but most of all, of undying gratitude. I wondered if it came from a voice actress or if it was artificially produced. Their death is not your ending. Their death is not your ending. Their death is not your ending.

I heard the ad play what felt like a million times after my father-in-law's death. It even displayed on my retinal scanners as I brushed my teeth. It flashed on my work screen during break. I could recite all the statistics, 91.5% of all clients report gaining closure. The testimonial of a veteran's widow was etched in my mind.

"It gave me the chance to say goodbye," she said before tears started to roll perfectly down her cheeks. A man in a uniform stood behind her; he radiated soft heavenly light. He cried too.

They proclaimed themselves to be an innovative new company that "will forever change and improve the way mankind deals with death." Truthfully, there was no such thing as a new company under the cartel of the mega corps. Go up the ladder and you'll find a subsidiary of a subsidiary of a subsidiary of a subsidiary…

Strangely, before the ad played, I had never heard of them. Friends, relatives, colleagues, no one ever mentioned Attis Grief Services. I suppose I never asked or mentioned it to them either. It was a strange thing to bring up.

Me and my wife never spoke of it but she must have been bombarded with even more messages. Eventually the ads tapered off, replaced by ones extolling the virtues of implanting an enhanced learning chip in my daughter's brain.

However, that morning as we ate breakfast my wife announced, "I'm going to Attis Grief Services at noon."

"Attis? You mean the hologram…"

"Yes… Attis Grief Services," she sheepishly replied. "I've thought about it a lot. Really thought about it, I mean." Her eyes were fixed on her plate of half-eaten eggs.

"I understand," I replied. My wife continued to stare at her eggs. "Do you want me to go with you or…"

"Do you want to go?"

She raised her head up and looked at me for a moment. I nodded. She nodded back. We continued our breakfast.

I was surprised; it had been nine months. For the first week, she sobbed every night while I held her tight. After that, save for the usual bouts of melancholy, she appeared fine. I honestly thought she had moved on. Healed.

The truth be told, I was uncomfortable with the idea. The concept of bringing back the dead even if it was just a hologram of them seemed morbid and distasteful. But I supposed I should support her. Who was I to tell another person how they should mourn?

"Are you sure seven days will be sufficient?" the young attendant at Attis asked. She had the face of a woman glowing with youth but the air of someone much wiser than either of us.

"I… I… believe… Yes. Yes. A week is enough." The attendant nodded with great respect. "But my father was born in 2021. So, he was eleven when the Guardian Safety Act was passed. Will that…"

"I understand, ma'am. The formative years give us great insight to an individual but the other 70 years of data in your father's memory implant is more than sufficient to produce an accurate replication."

Replication. They carefully used that word instead of replacement. In any case, my wife appeared relieved. She looked at me but my brow was furrowed deeply. I was wondering how to explain all this to our six-year-old daughter, Joan.

"Don't worry sir, it's all in the handbook," the young attendant said like she read my mind. They trained her well. Her smile looked as radiant as the flowers that bloomed behind her.

All three of us sat on the couch while we waited for the machine's act of necromancy. Joan watched us with curiosity while my wife and I sat utterly still. She swung her little legs gently up and down the couch while ours remained locked tight.

The machine was our hologram emitter. It's green light was on but it gave no other indication it was performing something utterly extraordinary.

Away from our sight, an artificial intelligence was merging with my father-in-law's database. His memories, behaviors, thought patterns, all were being pulled down from The Clouds back onto Earth. Our home detected our nervousness and offered us a cup of hot cocoa infused with small traces of sedatives. I was tempted to accept it but I wanted my senses fully attuned.

Then it happened. Attis' soft little jiggle played. A flash of light erupted from our emitter. My dead father-in-law materialized before us.

He was wearing his favorite outfit, a simple old collared shirt with slacks. He was light blue and translucent. I could see a faded image of the living room through his stomach. A faint glow radiated around him.

It was ethereal. He appeared to be a ghost. But I couldn't blame Attis for that, we were median-class and couldn't afford the fancy full-color holographic emitters.

"Dad? Daddy?" my wife said cautiously. She remained guarded in her seat.

"Ellie?" he responded. Though I could literally see through his eyes, I observed the pain and longing in them. The very way he pronounced her name. The twitch of his bushy brow. His soft exhalations. It made my heart drum, my breathes were vacuumed. It had just been nine months but I had forgotten so much.

It was so real.

An image flashed in my mind. It was him in the casket, eyes closed, arms rested gently by his sides. People at funerals always say "I can't believe they're gone. They look like they're sleeping." I never got that. It was always obvious to me. Dead is dead.

"Is that you?" Ellie asked in a throaty whisper.

"Yes, it's me. It's me. I-I'm so s-sorry… I… I… It's me," he said.

He looked old; he felt old. My wife chose him to be old. To appear as he did the few days before his death.

I looked at Ellie but I could not parse what she was feeling. Her eyes swept the projected image of her deceased father. Up and down. Up and down. Again and again and again.

A silence passed over us. We all remained locked in our place, paralyzed, including him. I would have presumed it was glitch but his expression of pain kept evolving. His sad regret palpated the air.

"Pop-Pop?" my daughter asked suddenly. The guidebook had advised us to keep the conversation short for children ages seven and below. "No need to complicate matters," the soothing voice instructed. "Their attention will be quickly diverted elsewhere."

Ellie bolted up from her seat and rushed towards him.

She hugged her father but all she grasped was the air. Her arms and body went through his. I thought this was the moment the illusion would be shattered, when reality snatched the veil. But she held on.

He put his own translucent blue hands over her. He 'stroked' her hair lovingly.

"I'm here. I'm here, Ellie. I'm here."

Ellie sobbed. She remained locked in this unreal embrace but she sobbed. It was hard for me to look at.

"How about we give Mommy some space, sweetie," I told Joan as I gently ushered her out of the room.

"I thought you said Pop-Pop's gone, Daddy?" she asked. She did not seem very bewildered. The question was posed in the most fleeting manner. I sighed as 'the handbook', appeared on my retinal display.

I turned to take one last look at father and daughter. While my wife's tears wet her cheeks and stained her dress, her father's droplets of lights faded into oblivion.

My holographic father-in-law sat across from me while we ate dinner together. Joan and I joined him and Ellie after they had both dried their tears. But when he saw his little granddaughter, he sobbed all over again. So much crying. I suppose since he was a hologram his tears were infinite.

In any case, he took a 'seat' at the table while we ate together. He could not eat with us of course, but there was an awkward moment where Ellie wasn't sure if she should set a plate for him anyway, as courtesy.

He laughed and said, "Don't worry. I'm not hungry. I don't think I can be."

He set his glowing blue eyes on us as we ate, flicking from Ellie to Joan and occasionally to me. A wistful smile played on his translucent lips. His brow was creased in joyful bewilderment. I could hear him taking a deep breath, I was sure he was going to cry again.

"Now, no more crying Dad, we've spent all afternoon doing that," Ellie ordered him in a stern tone.

"Yes! Don't cry, Pop-Pop!" Joan chimed in.

"I suppose I've been blubbering enough" he said as he rubbed his eyes and sighed. I observed his movements closely. They were so precise. Spectacular.

He caught my gaze and I quickly averted my eyes. I searched for a distraction.

"You know, Rickon James did actually beat Vaz for the Championship. Looks like your prediction came through," I told him.

"Told you so, didn't I?" he said with a wink. "But you know, I somehow already know that. They must have put that information in my brain somehow." He gave a casual shrug.

"What's it like?" Joan suddenly asked. It was the question both adults were too scared to ask.

"Well I... it's well... I can't exactly..." he started and stopped. "I feel like something's missing. No, more like I know something's missing but not in a bad way. I know I don't actually have a body right now. But it just doesn't, it doesn't even feel like I don't, yet I know I don't and it's... I don't think I have the words to describe it actually."

"Okay! That happens to me too!" Joan said happily.

"But there should be no more discussion on that. I want you all to treat me as you always have. Nothing's changed!" he declared.

The following days passed quicker than I thought they would, and my father-in-law acted as he did during his previous visits. He laughed as he watched old holopics, grumbled at the sorry state of the world and played silly games with my daughter. We avoided each other. The only exception was that he was confined here, inside this house. However, that was in line with his previous visits.

He always had a very peculiar habit. He would walk about our home like it was the city. He entered each room like he stepped into a new neighborhood. He would go about looking over each item in the room closely, whether it was the lamp or a discarded sock.

I was especially annoyed by the way he seemed to peer at my collection of awards from work. He probed and caressed them with his eyes before giving a long firm nod, like something in his mind was just confirmed. I had an insurmountable urge to yell at him to please respect our privacy. But I never did.

"He's just an old man with nothing better to do," Ellie would say. Her tone would be a strange mixture of guilt and defiance.

This time, he had the added advantage of being able to walk through walls. I dreaded the moment his blue glowing figure would emerge out of our bedroom walls. But he never did.

He roamed the hallways of our home in his traditional manner. I don't think it was a deliberate choice, I think he simply forgot.

We all forgot.

I forgot he was blue and transparent. My mind would somehow fill in the blanks of the missing parts of him, the color of his skin, the solidity of his figure. I would look at him sometimes and suddenly be engulfed in a wave of shock.

One evening, my daughter dropped her toy on the floor as she ran gleefully around the house. It was a pink rabbit.

"Oh! You're a clumsy one, pumpkin! Don't worry! Pop-Pop'll get it!" he proclaimed.

He had been playfully chasing her around the house. He wearily bent down and tried to scoop the toy up. His blue hands phased through it.

He tried again. Then again. The pink rabbit remained still on the floor. He looked up for a moment. The expression on his face was one of unfathomable confusion.

Then, he 'slapped' his forehead and gave a big hearty chuckle.

"Of course that's not going to work! Of course! Of course…" he said with a shake of the head. He flashed me a knowing grin.

I returned an awkward smile.

My daughter picked up the pink rabbit and began running wild again. He resumed the chase. Their laughter echoed throughout the house.

There were also 'the sessions."

For the most part, Ellie treated him as she always did. She even asked what he wanted for breakfast every morning, though he would always decline. But they would talk like they never did before.

They huddled in Ellie's study and engaged in long private conversations. It was there they acknowledged one of them was dead and the other was alive.

It would happen spontaneously, in the evening, afternoon, whenever. We would even be in mid-conversation when Ellie would suddenly decide it was time.

"I'm ready to meet with you now, Dad," Ellie would say. Her tone was like that of a receptionist announcing an appointment.

"Thank you," he would respond and follow her dutifully to the study.

I only had the barest hints of what went on in there. The unloading of past regrets, the telling of tales untold, the most naked of confessions, all this occurred no doubt but I was not part of it.

"Did you know my father actually saw the Rivet Bomb drop over New Orleans? He told me today he was stationed in Louisiana when it happened," Ellie told me one night as we lay in bed.

He was out there somewhere on 'sleep mode' in our guest room.

"No, I didn't know that," I said.

"I didn't know that either," she responded. I waited for her to continue but she avoided my gaze and turned over. She guarded this tale and others, held them close inside. I was isolated from the renewed intimacy between daughter and father.

Ellie used to tell me things about her father. Those 'sessions' were always just like this, in the middle of the night as we lay together on the bed. Her frustrations, her disappointment, her anger towards him became my own.

I feared those moments, those feelings would wash away. This new version of him would layer over everything else.

But then I reprimanded myself for being so selfish, so self-absorbed. I thought about my own parents and whether I would resurrect them.

They both died together in an eco-terrorist attack years ago. The bombs vaporized them so there was nothing left, not even ashes. It was a few months after I married Ellie. I was wracked with anxiety. Not because of their deaths; well, not directly.

I showed no emotion when I heard the news. I showed no emotion at their funeral. I showed no emotion in my most private moments when there was no one to watch or judge me.

Ellie thought I was suppressing a storm of grief, she was worried about me. I was worried she would realize there was something hideously wrong with me.

I loved my parents. They were fine people. They did their best to raise me within their limited means. They were kind and caring. They gave me everything they could hope to give. They were fine people. I loved them but I did not mourn them.

I couldn't.

When I was young, much younger, just entering my precinct's Academy, my aunt died. She was exposed to radiation when the local aeonic reactor suffered a meltdown. I was very close with her, she was more like a sister to me. We were close in age so it was always funny to me that I called her Aunt Joan, it was so oddly formal.

I almost collapsed on the hospital floor when I saw what happened to her. The rapid cellular degeneration deformed her completely.

A representative of the corporation that owned the aeonic reactor informed us they would cover all the medical costs.

"We're utilizing the most advanced medical technology for the healing process," he assured us. He said those words with the deepest and most unwavering sincerity.

Their technology stretched her life for another six months. I dropped out of the Academy just to be with her. Every day, I would sit next to her bed and read to her but inevitably I would break down sobbing as I listened to her anguished breathing through the machines.

By the end of it, I am not exaggerating when I say she was a skeleton.

Wretched pale skin draped over brittle bones. It was Saran Wrap thin. The machines had healed some parts of her but were powerless against the raw force of entropy. They were just applying duct tape on the shipwreck that was her body. Her appearance was an utter rejection of life.

When she died, I drowned.

I mourned so hard for her that I wondered if that was why I did not mourn my parents. Did I give away all my tears? Was there nothing left?

I imagined her as a hologram. My Aunt Joan. A glowing blue and translucent version of her but young and beautiful, not the misshapen shell that haunted my dreams. My heart drummed at the vision. She looked like an angel.

Didn't I beg for the chance to have her, to see her again as she was once before? To have her just answer me once as she lay there on the edge of death?

When my daughter was born, the first thought I had was that if only she could have met her namesake. Now that I have the opportunity, could I resurrect my Aunt Joan?

This time I had no answer to that question.

It was late at night when I found him whispering to my daughter. His glowing blue lips spilled unknown words into her ear. She giggled conspiratorially. He appeared to me to be both Hamlet's father and uncle.

"It's late. Go to bed, sweetie," I told my daughter.

"Goodnight, Pop-Pop," she said with a cute kiss on his glowing blue cheek. She was just touching light and air but she didn't care, just like her mother.

Once she was gone, he let out a long weary sigh.

"You don't have to be afraid of me you know," he said.

"I'm not," I responded.

"Oh, really now?" he smiled in amusement. "Here I thought that since I'm dead, we could finally be honest with each other."

He waited. I looked closely at him. The hologram of him. Dead at 91, he collapsed in the bathroom of his home when his mechanical heart malfunctioned. It wasn't that big a surprise.

He was living life on an extension after his original biological heart failed. It was sickening to me how quickly he jumped to install the replacement. All his life he railed against the immorality of cybernetics but then…

He continued to wait for me. He looked so 'paternal', filled with arrogant wisdom and understanding. Again, I marveled at the accuracy of it all. I wondered about the inside of him.

They simulated this, but could they simulate that? Could he feel his mechanical heart beating? Could he feel the nanobots inside that struggled to repair his aging body?

"I have no confession for you," I lied.

He gave another long weary sigh.

"Son, you are a fine person and you've been a wonderful husband to my little Ellie. You have, and I thank you for that from the bottom of my heart. You really are a fine person. But you know what your problem is? You just…"

"Shut down all holographic projections," I commanded my home.

He evaporated. Nowhere to be seen.

I took over the seat he was 'sitting' on. It was cold to the touch.

The next day as the sun rose, the machine summoned him once more. Neither of us mentioned the previous night's incident.

We were back at Attis' offices after the week was done to officially terminate the contract. The day before, Ellie had one final session with her father. Both went into her study but only she came out. We spent the night without him.

My daughter noted his absence.

"Where's Pop-Pop, Mommy?" Joan asked.

"His visit's over, sweetie. He's gone," was all Ellie said.

"Okie," Joan responded, and continued fiddling with her dinner.

In the middle of the night, I looked at Ellie's sleeping face. She looked impervious to the world around her. Her dream must have been of oak and mountains.

"Are you sure you would like to terminate the service, ma'am? We offer a three-day extension if you sign up for another week," said the attendant. It was a different person yet she was identical in every way.

"No, I'm quite sure," Ellie responded. She was resolute. The attendant nodded with great respect.

As we sat there waiting, I looked at my wife and wondered. No, I ached. I ached to know what he said to her that last time. What could a father say to a daughter to give her peace? I wanted her to tell me, so my own daughter wouldn't do the same. Resurrect a me who was not me. But again, was I being selfish? After all, who was I to tell another person how they should mourn.

If a ghost of me was what my daughter needed, why should it matter? I would be dead. Nothing but ashes. No thoughts, no memories, no emotions, no actions, nothing. The hologram would be more alive than me.

"Alright, the contract has been ended, ma'am. Is there anything else I can help you with?" the attendant asked.

Ellie just said "No."

Just as we got up to leave, the youthful attendant looked at me and asked, "What about you, sir? Our data indicates that you have experienced no recent deaths of relatives or close friends. However, our services have been rated as highly efficient and therapeutic in processing past unresolved grief."

I paused for a moment. I remembered my parents, the ones I could not mourn, gone so suddenly and violently. I remembered my Aunt Joan, the haunting sound of her shallow breathing as she was hooked up with all manner of monstrous machines. I then remembered Ellie's father; I'd been wondering what he wanted to say to me that night before I shut him off. What great wisdom did he want to impart to me? What was my problem?

"I think I prefer my deaths unresolved, keeps them alive in my head somehow," I answered. I looked at my wife. She nodded and I nodded back.

The attendant flashed her brilliantly bright smile again and said "We all deal with death in our own special way. Thank you for using Attis Grief Services. In case you change your mind and wish to restart the service in the future, don't worry! They'll always be in The Cloud."

While we were being transported back to our home, I told my wife about my parents. The emptiness I felt, the guilt of not being able to mourn. When we arrived home, I sat my daughter down and told her about her Great-Aunt Joan. I told Joan about her life and her death. The happiness, the pain and everything in between.

Feng Gooi was born and raised in the sunny tropical island of Penang, Malaysia but is currently in snowy Buffalo, New York studying for his Masters in Mental Health Counseling. He enjoys staring out the window while eating Doritos and is an easy prey for salesmen of all sorts.

Isn't Your Daughter Such a Doll

Tobi Ogundiran

1

"**Je m'appelle Ralia,**" said the girl beside Celine for the umpteenth time, "*Je suis Nigerianne. Je suis une fille, comme toi.*"

Celine ignored her, put a finger to her tongue to wet it and turned over the page she was reading. Of course she wasn't *really* reading, but not for lack of trying. Her eyes glazed over the page, the words a blur of black. She wondered why her mother thought she could ever be friends with this girl. This girl who kept introducing herself over and over, undaunted by Celine's coldness towards her, determined to make her acquaintance. She looked across the park to where her mother sat, chatting animatedly with her friend in rapid Yoruba, and wondered when she would be done. Celine was bored already, and wanted to go home.

"*Je m'appelle Ralia –*" the girl called Ralia began, but Celine was having none of it.

"Just shut up!" she snapped and stood up to leave.

"Wait!" Ralia cried, gripping Celine's arm "Don't leave."

Celine turned to look at her, eyes flashing with annoyance. "So you speak English."

"Yes," said Ralia.

"But you keep speaking French to me," said Celine, a little bewildered, "and the same words."

Ralia shrugged sheepishly. "We're in Paris," she mumbled, "if I knew you didn't understand French –"

"I understand French." Celine cut in.

"But you don't reply to me."

Celine cocked her brows. "That's because I wasn't interested in talking to you."

"Oh…"

They stood there in silence for a few moments, and Celine realized with a start that this was the first time she had really looked at Ralia. She had long beautiful lashes, her hair collected in twin braids.

Ralia's eyes lit up. "Do you want to be friends? I can do things. Interesting things. We'll have so much fu –"

Celine screwed up her nose. "No. I don't need friends –"

"Yes, you do," said Ralia, taking Celine's hands in hers, and there was something about the way their hands fit that was perfect, as though they were made for each other. Celine liked it. She didn't want to withdraw her hands as she was wont to do when in contact with strangers. Yes, she needed friends. Yes, she was lonely. That was why her mother introduced her to Ralia, a good fine black girl who was Nigerian and would understand her. And there was something about Ralia …

"Ok," she said finally, "let's be friends."

2

They became fast friends, Ralia and Celine. They became sisters. You could almost always find them hand in hand, skipping down the streets of Paris and singing their favourite song. They wore each other's clothes, braided each other's hair and slept in the same bed, hugging each other tightly. Celine's parents were immensely pleased. Her father (who was French and owned his own bakery) delighted her and Ralia with sweets and other confectioneries whenever he returned from work – much to the chagrin of her mother (who was Nigerian and curated a book salon), who argued that he was spoiling them too much.

"*Non, ma cherie,*" he would reply, "let them be as happy as they can be."

One chilly autumn evening, Celine lay in her bed reading her favourite book, while Ralia skipped on the bed until she was exhausted and finally flopped down next to Celine.

"What are you reading?" she asked, peering over Celine's shoulder.

"*The Hunchback of Notre-Dame.*"

"Oh," said Ralia, falling back on the bed, "I've read that a thousand times."

Celine grunted in reply, engrossed in the book. She enjoyed the bright illustrations in this edition, and was particularly fascinated with the hideous hump on Quasimodo's back.

Ralia, seeing that she was being ignored, reached over and snatched the book, jumping off the bed before Celine could snatch it back.

"Give it back!" Celine cried, springing off the bed.

"No," said Ralia, "it's a stupid book."

"It's *NOT* a stupid book!" Celine cried in defiance.

"Yes. It. Is," said Ralia, sticking out her tongue. "You've read it several times already."

"So have you," Celine countered.

Ralia gave a sugary smile. "You don't see me reading it now, do you?"

"I don't care!" Celine cried, and she lunged for Ralia. But Ralia was faster; she opened the window and threw out the book. They both watched it draw a parabola in the overcast sky, the wind ripping its pages like a savage dog, before it dropped down in bits and pieces to the Parisian streets below.

Celine screamed, a familiar rage rising up in her. She charged at Ralia, who was laughing. She scratched her, yanked at her hair, kicked her, and screamed so loudly that both her parents broke into the room, their faces masks of worry.

"Celine – CELINE!"

But there was no reasoning with her. Her father lifted her easily with one arm, and it was not until her mother threatened to smack her to the sky and back that she grew calm and stopped thrashing. Ralia lay on the floor, a battered, trembling heap. She hadn't protected herself at all, she hadn't even fought back. Celine hung limply in her father's hands, coming slowly to her senses, wondering if the book was worth so much that it caused her to violently attack her friend.

Celine watched her mother rush over to Ralia's aid. She gently guided her into a sitting position and brushed the tangles of her hair away from her face. Ralia's face was barely recognizable; it was swollen and streaked with blood where Celine had scratched her.

"Jesu Christi," said her mother.

"*Mon Dieu*," echoed her father.

"I'm sorry," said Celine in a small voice. She wriggled free of her father's grip and went over to Ralia. She stretched out a hand – to help, to comfort, she didn't know – but Ralia flinched away, shrinking into the wall and the curtains, and it was a knife through Celine's heart.

"I want to go home," sobbed Ralia. "I want to go home."

3

Celine did not see Ralia for two weeks and she very nearly went mad. She hung out in their favourite park in the hopes that Ralia would come skipping so she could apologize profusely to her. But Ralia never showed up. It struck Celine as odd that in the several months they had known each other, she had never been to Ralia's house. She didn't even know who her parents were, or what school she went to. She begged her mother, who had introduced her to Ralia, for her address. Surely she would know. But her mother merely pursed her lips and shook her head and said, "When Ralia's ready to see you, she'll show herself."

Her father still brought her sweets and cookies every day from work, but now that Ralia was not here to share them with her, Celine had absolutely no appetite for them. Once, as she walked down the street with her mother, she caught sight of Ralia dancing and skipping merrily to the tunes of a street saxophonist. Celine let go of her mother's hand and raced to her friend, sweeping her up in a crushing hug.

"Oh Ralia, Ralia! I'm so happy to see you! I'm sorry –!"

"*Qui es-tu?*" asked the girl, flustered. "*Qui es Ralia?*"

"Oh, sorry…"

It wasn't Ralia. The tears came unbidden to her eyes, and Celine stood there in the middle of the street. Her mother's firm but gentle hand pulled her away from the bewildered girl and saxophonist. She led Celine to the railing overlooking the River Seine below.

"I do believe you've learnt your lesson, Celine," she said softly, wiping the tears that coursed down Celine's cheeks, "it doesn't matter what has been done to you – never *ever* lash out like that. We're not animals, thank God, so we shouldn't behave like one."

"I know, mama," said Celine, "but where is Ralia? I want to apologize."

"I will speak to her father," said her mother, "I'm sure Ralia would love to see you too."

That night, as Celine rocked herself to sleep, she heard her door open and caught a whiff of Ralia's familiar scent. She sprang out of the bed and swept Ralia up in a hug. She held her at arm's length to study her face; the scratch marks were still there, and though they were healing, they would leave black marks across her face once they had healed completely. A wave of guilt washed over Celine.

"I'm sorry, Ralia! I'm *so* sorry sorry sorry –"

"It's fine," said Ralia, "I'm sorry too. I shouldn't have thrown out your book. I was stupid –"

"No, I was stupid! I shouldn't have –"

"No, *I* was –"

They burst out laughing. A warm feeling of contentment spread over Celine.

"Look, I bought you a new one." Ralia produced a gift pack from the folds of her skirt and withdrew from it a sparkling new copy of *The Hunchback of Notre-Dame*.

They fell asleep in each other's arms.

4

By the next morning, under the bright rays of the sun, Celine could see that Ralia was limping. It was a slight limp, barely noticeable, but it was there alright. Celine initially decided to ignore it, but as the day progressed, Ralia's limp became even more pronounced, so that she was forced, eventually, to voice concern.

"Did I do this to you?" she asked tentatively.

"What?" asked Ralia, a little distracted. She was trying to catch a pigeon.

"Your leg. You're limping."

"Oh, this!" said Ralia, laughing. She lunged and closed her hands around the unsuspecting pigeon which promptly gave a loud squawk, struggling to free itself. It soon gave up, realizing the futility of its efforts. "I twisted my ankle when I jumped from the bell tower. I always land in an easy crouch, but this last time I was distracted. So, I twisted my ankle. It'll be fine."

Celine wasn't quite sure she heard correctly. "You *jumped* from the bell tower?"

Ralia gave her a sly look, a light smile playing on her lips. She reached into her pocket and brought out some breadcrumbs ,which she began to feed to the grateful pigeon. "Yes. I've been jumping off the bell tower ever since I read *The Hunchback.*"

Celine searched Ralia's face for hints of mischief. There were none. "But... the tower is very high... how haven't you died?"

"I simply believed," said Ralia. She crouched and let go of the pigeon. But it had imprinted on her and wouldn't move, no matter how hard she shooed. "It's like flying, really. The best feeling in the world. You simply climb up there, believe you can do it, and then let go." She smiled at Celine's perplexed look. "I told you I can do things. I can show you of course, if you like."

Yes, she liked. She was curious as to how one could survive a fall of over 300 feet.

5

"Do you want to hear a story?" Ralia asked.

They were back in Celine's room. Celine sat between Ralia's legs, her head tilted backwards as Ralia braided her hair.

"Yeah."

"It's a Nigerian folk tale," said Ralia, "my father loves to tell me Nigerian tales to remind me of my roots – does your mother tell you folk tales?"

"No," said Celine. She knew very little about Nigeria, except the fact that it was hot and her relatives were so numerous it was hard to place who was who. She had seen the photo albums. The lot of them – seventy or so – grinning in spite of the sun's glare.

Ralia gave a dramatic sigh. "You poor thing. Well, it's lucky you have me. So the tale begins like this:

"In a little village called Esie, there lived a wicked king. He was rich and powerful and very unkind. The villagers feared him. Anyone who tried to stand up to him always disappeared without trace, and so the villagers learned with time not to complain, regardless of the harsh living conditions. There was very little food. The king took it all – and not that there was famine or anything like that – no. He just wanted them to suffer. He liked to watch them suffer."

"He was very wicked," Celine remarked.

"Yes," Ralia agreed, visibly pleased. "He took all the best lands for himself, all the best girls – he had a very large harem of beautiful virgin girls." (Celine giggled.) "Anyway, one day he went about the village as usual, seeking the finest girls to collect for his harem, when he found this girl by the stream. She was singing. Her voice was magic and the king fell in love immediately. He took her and decided to make her his queen, not just place her in the harem like the others. The girl, of course, was upset. She didn't want to leave her family and friends and spend her days locked up in the palace. But her family begged her not to cause any trouble, because the king always made trouble-makers disappear. Did she want them to disappear? Did she? She answered no and that was that. She was taken to the palace and was made queen.

"The palace was large, and she had thousands of servants who served her and attended to her needs, but she was lonely. Even though this wicked and terrible king did his best to be kind to her, she still felt unhappy. Even though she was generally free to roam the palace, she was never allowed to leave and soon it became clear that she was a prisoner. The only time she was alone was at night, and so in the nights, she started to explore the palace, seeking for an escape.

"That was how she came across the door with no lock."

"A door with no lock…" Celine repeated in a hushed, dramatic whisper. She tried to envision a door with no lock and the vision of a wall rose in her mind.

"A door with no lock," Ralia repeated. "It was a magic door and it always changed positions. This night it was here, another night it was there, and the girl enjoyed roaming the palace every night, trying to find where the door would appear. Every night she found it, she grew more and more excited, until she was no longer content with just finding the door. She wanted to *open* it, to see what was behind it. She was convinced the way to escape and freedom was behind it."

Celine turned to face Ralia now, her eyes wide with excitement. "Did she open it?"

Ralia smiled. "The door sensed she wanted to enter and spoke to her. It said, 'I am a door, my name is Door. I am a protector of the secrets within.' The girl answered, 'I am a girl, I am the Queen. Open, Door and admit me in!' and the door swung open."

Celine clapped and whooped with glee. "And what did she find!" she asked breathlessly.

"Hundreds and hundreds of small stone sculptures," said Ralia, "the girl realized with horror that they were the villagers who had disappeared, turned to stone sculptures by the king!" (Celine clapped a hand over her mouth). "She ran out of that room and roused the palace, screaming at the top of her voice of the atrocities behind the vanishing Door. The news of what the king had done soon spread around the village and all the villagers, in their fury, marched to the palace to kill the king."

"*Yes!*" Celine whooped.

"But the king fled and was never heard from again," Ralia finished. "Till this day, the Door remains in Esie, changing positions every night, hiding the hundreds of statues behind it."

"Wow," Celine breathed. Dusk had fallen; long shadows fell across the room. She could see the Door before her. The door without a lock, hiding humans turned to stone. "But it's not true, is it? It's a folk tale."

Ralia shrugged. Just then, Celine's mother called from the kitchen. "Dinner, my dears!"

Ralia slapped Celine awake. "Do you want to see me jump?"

"What?" asked Celine, her eyes still groggy with sleep.

"Do you want to see me jump from the bell tower?"

"Oh …" she sat up. "Yeah!"

"Come on."

They got dressed quickly, donning warm coats to protect from the autumn chill. Within minutes, they'd snuck out of the house and were bounding along the street to the bell tower, under the bright glare of a full moon. Celine had the distant feeling that she was in a dream and would wake up soon. She'd never snuck out of the house before, much less at night. And now she was going to watch her best friend jump off a tower to certain death. For surely no living person could survive that fall... without a parachute. Of course that was it! Ralia had a parachute.

"You're going to use a parachute, aren't you?" asked Celine excitedly, hoping Ralia's answer was going to be in the affirmative. Nothing like that. Ralia merely looked at her and shook her head.

Celine was getting scared now. What if Ralia actually jumped? Without a parachute. She was going to die. Was she really just going to stand there and watch her friend die?

"I'm scared, Ralia."

"Don't be a scaredy-cat," came the curt reply.

They'd arrived at the foot of the tower. The colossal structure stood stark and forbidding against the night sky.

Ralia took off her bag. "There are three hundred and eighty-seven stairs to the top," she said, "I'll try to run as fast as possible. You wait here and watch me as I jump."

"But –" Celine began, but her friend was gone.

Modupe stood up from the chair in her study and stretched. It had been a long day. Apart from the brief hour or two when she left to make dinner for her daughter Celine and her husband Pierre, she had remained holed up in her study all day, translating the last pages of *The Secret Lives of Baba Segi's Wives* to French for the ladies of her book club. A fine mix of ladies, they were. Immigrants who'd married French. And so, they spent their time reading the literature of their countries, seeking to immerse themselves in each other's experiences. She cracked her knuckles, removed her glasses and waited for her laptop to shut down before switching off the lights and exiting the study.

It was 2:00 a.m. Her husband was already fast asleep, and so was her daughter. Her beautiful little girl. Raising a child was no small feat, especially one as troubled as her daughter. She had suffered severely from depression, the poor thing. She'd gone through almost four months of not speaking at all, scaring both Pierre and her. All she needed was a companion, the benign psychologist had told her, perhaps a brother or a sister? But she and Pierre had been unable to provide her with a sibling, and it was not for lack of trying. The first time had been easy – she'd gotten pregnant with Celine almost immediately after their marriage. But now, try as they could, she just wasn't getting pregnant. And Celine was sliding deeper and deeper into herself.

"Buy her a doll," her friend had advised, "girls are good with dolls. I bought my daughter one – maybe it will help your daughter."

But Modupe had been skeptical. Teaching a child to enjoy the company of dolls and not real humans? How was that going to help her in the long run? She thought of taking her to Nigeria, maybe a change of scenery would do her good. But she had vowed never to return to Nigeria, never to return to Esie.

She still had nightmares about the disappearing door and the stone sculptures...

And so, she got her daughter a doll. She searched long and hard for a good dollmaker who made quality dolls of girls of colour. She didn't want some random white doll with blue eyes that didn't look anything like her daughter. Imagine her elation, therefore, when in the newspapers she finally found a Nigerian dollmaker based just on the outskirts of Paris, who specialized in quality handcrafted dolls. She called to order one instantly, giving specifications as to how it would look from the skin colour, down to the hairstyle, and even the pre-recorded phrases in French: *Hi. My name is Ralia. I am Nigerian. I am a little girl, just like you.*

The doll came... and it looked uncannily like her daughter. If Modupe was honest, the resemblance unnerved her, tickled at something buried in the deepest recesses of her mind. But Pierre never saw the resemblance, and neither did Celine. And her worries all but vanished when Celine took to the doll with much glee.

Celine loved the doll and both Modupe and Pierre were grateful! She went everywhere with the doll, even insisted on feeding it her father's confectioneries. It was odd, admittedly, but she was a little girl who had found a companion in a doll. A doll that helped her out of her depression. So, Modupe and Pierre overlooked it. She would grow out of it eventually –

Until that night when she attacked the doll in a fit of rage. Modupe had been scared to find that her daughter had so much destruction in her; the doll was in a bad shape and had to be shipped back to the dollmaker for repairs. She would have driven down to the shop herself to expedite the process, but the dollmaker had insisted she post it instead. She realized then that she had never met the dollmaker, even upon purchase. Odd, but Modupe had dealt with numerous eccentric creatives to know they all had their quirks.

The envelope on the mantelpiece jolted Modupe out of her reverie. How did it get here? Perhaps Pierre had placed it there so he wouldn't forget to take it to the post in the morning. She took the envelope and saw scrawled across the back a child's writing:

FROM MY DADDY

A lump appeared in Modupe's throat. Something wasn't right. With great trepidation, she ripped open the envelope to find a letter:

I am your husband; I am the king.

Isn't your daughter such a doll?

She flew from the living room up the stairs and into Celine's room. Celine was gone.

So was Ralia the doll.

Celine watched as Ralia materialized from behind the large bell, waving down at her. She shouted something, but she was too high up, and the wind carried her words away. Ralia spread out her hands and jumped.

Celine watched in pure terror as Ralia fell... or not. She wasn't falling; the wind carried her, tossed her about like paper, or a stray autumn leaf. She fell like a leaf. Zig. Zag. Zig. Zag. It was as though she were lighter than the air around her. As though she wasn't made of bones and blood and sinew –

Ralia dropped to the ground in a perfect crouch. "Well!" she exclaimed, clapping her hands excitedly. "What do you think?"

Celine looked, and looked, and looked... because this was Ralia, but then it *wasn't*. This wasn't the girl she knew… and yet it was.

Here was the truth in front of her, and she had always known it, hadn't she?

Hadn't she?

Ralia came over and took Celine's hand. Her hand was cool and smooth and the hardness of plastic.

"Did you like it?" she asked Celine. "I know you did. You can do it too; all you have to do is believe."

And then they were atop the bell tower, the beautiful city of Paris spread out before their eyes. And there was the bridge, the River Seine, the Eiffel Tower.

"Do you believe?" Ralia asked, her plastic eyes hard and unblinking.

"I believe," said Celine.

"Now look down. Do you see that man?"

Celine looked. Yes, yes, she saw the man. The man hiding in the shadows, he himself a shadow in his long trench coat.

"That is my daddy. He is waiting for us."

Celine turned to look at Ralia. This wasn't right. Everything was wrong. Everything! But she was past the point of no return.

"Close your eyes."

And then she was flying. Flying. Zig. Zag. Zig. Zag. She was lighter than the breeze. Her body was cool and smooth and plastic. But it was alright. Because she was flying.

He placed the two little dolls, the pretty little things, side by side. They were holding hands. That was good. He left them unperturbed and closed the lid of the box.

Tobi Ogundiran is a Nigerian writer of scary and fantastical stories, some of which have appeared in *The Dark, Beneath Ceaseless Skies,* and *FIYAH.* When he's not writing, you can almost always find him strumming on a guitar, trying to serenade that ever-elusive muse. He currently resides in Russia, where he's studying to become a doctor. He tweets @tobi_thedreamer

BECOME A PATRON

SHORELINE OF INFINITY HAS A *PATREON* PAGE AT

WWW.PATREON.COM/ SHORELINEOFINFINITY

ON *PATREON*, YOU CAN PLEDGE A MONTHLY PAYMENT FROM *AS LOW AS $1* IN EXCHANGE FOR *A COOL TITLE* AND A *REGULAR REWARD.*

ALL PATRONS GET AN *EARLY DIGITAL ISSUE* OF THE MAGAZINE QUARTERLY AND *EXCLUSIVE ACCESS* TO OUR PATREON MESSAGE FEED AND SOME GET *A LOT MORE.* HOW ABOUT THESE?

POTENT PROTECTOR SPONSORS A STORY EVERY YEAR WITH FULL CREDIT IN THE MAGAZINE WHILE AN *AWESOME AEGIS* SPONSORS AN ILLUSTRATION.

TRUE BELIEVER SPONSORS A *BEACHCOMBER COMIC* AND *MIGHTY MENTOR* SPONSORS A COVER PICTURE.

AND .... OUR HIGHEST HONOUR ... *SUPREME SENTINEL* SPONSORS A *WHOLE ISSUE* OF SHORELINE OF INFINITY.

CONER '17

ASK *YOUR FAVOURITE BOOK SHOP* TO GET YOU A COPY. WE ARE ON THE *TRADE DISTRIBUTION LISTS.*

R BUY A COPY *DIRECTLY* ROM OUR *ONLINE SHOP* AT

WW.SHORELINEOFINFINITY.COM

OU CAN GET AN *ANNUAL* UBSCRIPTION THERE TOO.

KINDLE FANS CAN GET SHORELINE FROM THE *AMAZON KINDLE STORE*

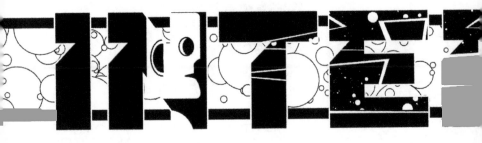

Raman Mundair is an Indian born, queer, disabled, writer, artist and activist based in Shetland and Glasgow. She is the award-winning author of *Lovers, Liars, Conjurers and Thieves, A Choreographer's Cartography, The Algebra of Freedom* (a play), and is the editor of *Incoming: Some Shetland Voices.*
Her work is socially and politically observant, bold, mischievous, cutting edge and potent with poetic imagery and integrity. She has performed and exhibited her artwork around the world. She presents the Intersectional Voices podcast and is the founder of EKTA - a Facebook intersectional feminist space.
Twitter: @MundairRaman Insta: @rmundair
anchor.fm/raman-mundair

T. L. Huchu's work has appeared in *Lightspeed Interzone, AfroSF, The Apex Book of World SF 5, Ellery Queen Mystery Magazine, Mystery Weekly, The Year's Best Crime and Mystery Stories 2016,* and elsewhere. He is the winner of a Nommo Award for African SFF, and has been shortlisted for the Caine Prize and the Grand prix de l'Imaginaire. His new fantasy novel *The Library of the Dead,* the first book in the Edinburgh Nights series, will be published by Tor Books in the US and UK in 2021. Find him @TendaiHuchu.

Stepping Through the Portal

Guest editors Raman Mundair and Tendai Huchu in conversation

Raman Mundair: I must admit, for a long time I thought sci-fi and speculative fiction wasn't for me. That the genre didn't include people like me. That the genre didn't accommodate or imagine Black and Brown people with the same freedom of possibility and creativity that it offered the rest of humanity. That it was a space full of androids, alien futures and anarchy. That changed when I started reading graphic novels and when I reread Ralph Ellison's *Invisible Man* and reframed the narrative. I'm interested in hearing about your relationship with sci-fi and speculative fiction. What drew you to it?

Tendai Huchu: **That is both interesting and a troubling feature of Western society which, since the Enlightenment, has been built around exclusion and** domination of the 'other'. I grew up in independent Zimbabwe watching *Star Trek* every Friday night on TV and reading dated pulp sci-fi classics in libraries that had been designed for white Rhodesian kids. I didn't necessarily see the canon through a racial lens and sci-fi was a foreign import we enjoyed alongside westerns and kung fu movies. As a result I am very comfortable with the idea that I am appropriating an alien artform by working within the genre and carving out my own niche there because, beyond ideas, the genre is fun and a great creative sandpit to play in for the modern writer.

RM: Your experience in Zimbabwe I think is echoed by many people of colour around the world and made me think of an FKA twigs lyric:

"I've never seen a hero like me in a sci-fi

So I wonder if your needs are even meant for me

I wonder if you think that I could never raise you up

I wonder if you think that I could never help you fly

Never seen a hero like me in a sci-fi"

What works in this genre are seminal to you? For me, as a woman of colour, Octavia Butler is a touchstone but I also count Charlotte Perkins Gilman's *Herland* as a favourite too.

TH: It's pretty interesting that you cite both Butler and Gilman who stand at opposite ends of the spectrum, given Gilman's appalling views on race. I've not read *Herland* but it's going on my to-read list. A lot of my favourite authors could be considered 'problematic' (isn't everyone once you get to know them?), but life would be pretty boring if we only read saints. I loved Samuel Delany's *Dhalgren*, which is stylistically and technically innovative and so out there it blew my mind in my twenties. I'd love to get your thoughts on how we navigate the past in the genre, as we have seen with Lovecraft's bust being replaced for the World Fantasy Awards, the James Tiptree Jr. Award renamed, and so on and so forth. Is there some way of reconciling great art[ists] with the pernicious ideologies they also espoused, which is something the modern reader has to think about?

RM: Ah, it's a tricky subject and the waters are shark infested. I navigate the past and these dangerous waters with caution. With trepidation. I definitely think that it's not one or the other, it's not binary. I am able to hold the fact that the artist is problematic, abhorrent even, alongside the fact that at one point their work held meaning for me. That aspects of their work shaped my thoughts and at the same time I am able to hold them accountable.

TH: **I'm sympathetic to that position because nuance and discernment are in short supply in this age when likes and retweets demand a certain kind of absolute clarity, no ifs or buts. It's only a few months in the year and we've already had two controversies from the other side of the pond (*American Dirt* and the Barnes & Noble Fifth Avenue book covers debacle). I would like to believe that in both those cases well-meaning people made creative decisions that were not intended to cause needless harm and/or offence and then the whole thing backfired. You and me are co-editing a BAME issue of this magazine, but in a true meritocracy this would be completely unnecessary. How then do you feel as an artist about being in this position? Is the work we are doing here truly meaningful or is it purely cosmetic, something to suit the general mood before the pendulum swings back, as it were?**

RM: My starting point for conversations around these issues is that we live in a deeply flawed world. One that is full of structural injustice. That is the reality. This issue is a small step in the right direction. It's an opportunity to reframe and amplify a different perspective. One that is frequently drowned out. As guest editors we are gatekeepers and these positions are rarely in our hands. Primarily because the publishing industry does not exist in a vacuum and has its role in maintaining the inequity that exists. That said, what we urgently need are allies that are willing to relinquish or share their power and platform in a meaningful way in order to challenge the status quo.

Raman: "As guest editors we are gatekeepers and these positions are rarely in our hands. Primarily because the publishing industry does not exist in a vacuum and has its role in maintaining the inequity that exists"

Since we began work on this, a very real dystopia and/or alternative world has emerged under the spectre of the coronavirus. We are generation lockdown, generation waiting-for-the-curve-to-flatten. It feels poignant to reflect on a genre that frequently uses the possibility of contagion to spark a narrative arc. Where do you feel this genre can take us, particularly writers of colour, given that we know that this virus has had a significant effect on people of colour around the world?

TH: **I really like what you say about living in a deeply flawed world and the need then to correct some of those imbalances where and when we can. There is no magic wand for this, and the real work of doing it is often unsexy; reaching out to people, one by one, making a small difference in your own little patch, that kind of thing. It's funny how when we came on board to do this magazine issue, the corona thing was something happening far away in China to other people. Life was going on as normal. We had our meeting and made our plans with a fair degree of certainty about things. Now it's all up in the air; you have conversations with friends/ family/colleagues but you can't be sure if they'll be there in** two, three week's time. But this sense of precariousness has always been embedded in works by writers of colour, particularly because of the arbitrary nature of living under colonialism or in conditions of slavery. I come from Zimbabwe, a country in which up to a quarter of the adult population lives with HIV/AIDS. Coronavirus in that matrix is just one more thing atop other ongoing disasters occuring there. Quite honestly I have no confidence that literature can even begin to address some of these things, not at such an early juncture. Not in 10, or even 20 years time. The greatest works of literature are often written long after the fact, as opposed to those written immediately in response to a particular event.

How have you found the experience of going through the slush pile for this issue? I'm thinking here not only of the pieces you chose but also the whole lot. Are there any pieces you may have turned down that you look back on and think, I might have missed one?

RM: I understand the value of letting things settle, to process fully before responding but believe that sometimes creativity can be an invaluable part of forming our response. This genre can be a tool and

Tendai: "I think speculative fiction since Mary Shelley has recognised how we sow the seeds of our own destruction"

means to explore and exorcise ideas and possibilities in innovative and playful ways. Adrienne Maree Brown in her blog recently addressed her anxiety around the current health pandemic through a speculative dialogue with a dinosaur. As an extinct species the dinosaur is in a unique position to enter into a discourse with the anxious author who fears the beginning of the end for humanity. The resulting tension between the two voices is interesting and creates an important space for airing a truth during these fear-filled times. This moment in our evolution where we have no definite timeline for the coronavirus and are held captive by it.

It was a privilege to read the poetry submissions for this issue and my choices stood out from the beginning. My original call-out asked for work that reflected on the possibility of new imagined creative futures. This request feels more relevant than ever and presents urgent questions: post this current world order what will we build? What will we create? What will we tolerate? What can we no longer afford to maintain?

TH: **I think it's certainly been clear the last few decades that we simply can't carry on as we have been doing. The dinosaur story by Brown which you mention sounds like a super-intriguing thought experiment. Of course, I think nature was kinder to dinosaurs in that they could not have known extinction was coming for them, and if the asteroid theory is correct then mercifully it wasn't even their fault. We on the other hand are responsible for, and conscious of, our own fuck-ups. The high-carbon economy which is threatening the delicate ecosystems we rely on for our existence, the numerous species we've driven to extinction just because we can, hell even this new virus is a result of our own actions. I think speculative fiction since Mary Shelley has recognised how we sow the seeds of our own destruction, but perhaps I digress too much here... I should stop now... When I was reading through the fiction slush, I saw a lot of brilliant stories. It made** my job really, really difficult. The sheer range of content was incredible and I certainly wish we'd had a few more slots available but ultimately I chose the stories which I thought would give the reader something genuinely fresh and insightful. And then during the editing process I was exposed to my own biases: for example, working with Zen Cho on her marvellous contribution 'Odette', she politely made me aware I'd gone through huge chunks of the story ironing out instances of Malaysian English because I assumed they were grammatically incorrect. Zen's really cool and gracious, and she saved me a lot of embarrassment here, but you can then imagine that surely there might be stories I missed out in the pile simply because I did not *get* what the author was doing as opposed to any real artistic failing on their part. I hope this shows that diversity can't really be fixed by having one or two brown faces in an organisation. Ultimately you need a whole pool of people working together on this, teaching and educating one another, so hopefully you create an inclusive culture which approximates a true meritocracy, because I believe what all writers want and deserve is a level playing field so they know when they send their work out there it gets a fair shot. We all get rejected and that's fine, but it stings when it comes because of your identity as opposed to the quality of your work. Perhaps you could round this conversation off, Raman, by maybe telling me what your hopes are for this issue and the incredible writers we are privileged to be publishing.

RM: Your sharing your experience of editing Zen Cho's work in Malaysian English reminded me of when I (briefly) taught in a university English department in England and had to fight for books in Indian English, patois and pidgin English to be recognised as legitimate texts of value and be included as part of the spectrum of literature in English. We're a long way off from being seen. We have far to go until embracing different voices as part of the canon becomes the norm or even as you say, to be recognised as talent by editorial gatekeepers, but I do think that sharing experiences, as you have, and having interventions like this will begin to make a difference.

We need change at all levels. We need change at all levels, and simultaneously – we need change when it comes to who gatekeeps, reviews, publishes, edits, promotes, teaches, canonises, reads and markets our work. We need to demand more. Challenge the status quo and current failure of imagination. The world feels sensitive to change right now in these delicate, fragile times. Let's use that. Bridge the gaps that failure of imagination has left. This issue, I hope, is a small step towards that.

I want to conclude with a quote from an Indian writer – Arundhati Roy, which surfaced in my social media recently, and although she is not specifically speaking about science fiction or speculative fiction, her words illuminate a truth:

> *"Historically, pandemics have forced humans to break with the past and imagine their world anew. This one is no different. It is a portal, a gateway between one world and the next.*
>
> *We can choose to walk through it, dragging the carcasses of our prejudice and hatred, our avarice, our data banks and dead ideas, our dead rivers and smoky skies behind us. Or we can walk through lightly, with little luggage, ready to imagine another world. And ready to fight for it."*

May we have the courage to step through the portal and remain ever-ready to imagine another world.

The Writer Reads:

Dream Babes, ed. Victoria Sin. I am completely blown away every time I read this shimmering swirl of a zine. It will remind you that imagination is infinite and saturated with potential.

Octavia's Brood, ed. adrienne maree brown and Walida Imarisha. An essential collection of intersectional, visionary short stories. If you're interested in speculative fiction's ability to empower and embolden—read it!

Transcendent 2, ed. Bogi Takács. A stellar collection of short stories that transcends cishet confines of gender, with many authors being BAME/POC.

—*Arianne Maki a speculative writer who facilitates a reading group on social justice and SF in Glasgow.*

The History of Japanese Science Fiction: from the 1930s to the 2010s

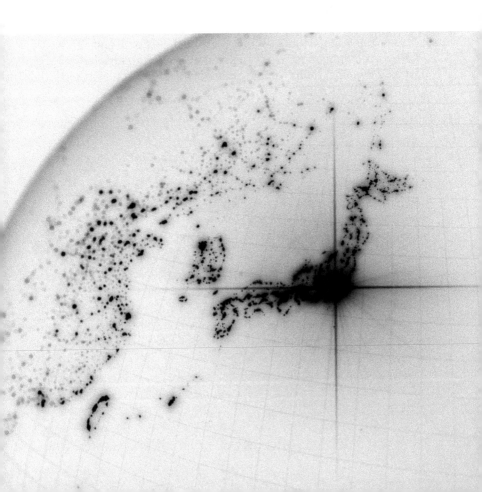

Atsushi Naito, Chiho Karafune, Hisashi Kujirai, Reisen Kawabata, Nao Hirami, Shinkyo Fujikawa, and Makoto Shirakawa

Hello all. We are the translator club Babel Uo, a society of amateur SF/F fans in Japan. Through translation and criticism, we introduce English-language SF/F short stories to a Japanese audience. Now we are pleased to be able to introduce the history of Japanese science fiction here in English, instead of our usual work.

First, we would like to thank our editor, Tendai Huchu, for this difficult and rewarding opportunity. This summer, we will be publishing our first issue. Impressed by his wonderful short story 'Njuzu', we contacted him to request the rights to translate and publish it in our journal. He not only kindly agreed to our offer but also suggested that we write an introduction to Japanese science fiction in Shoreline of Infinity.

While Japanese anime and manga are well known, Japanese SF/F in prose form is still not, except for the more widely read works of Haruki Murakami. But there is more to Japanese speculative fiction than just him alone. In this article, we will briefly summarise the history of Japanese science fiction for about 100 years and introduce some of the key authors. Most of the works featured in the text have been translated into English and are available on amazon. co.uk.

With more and more attention being paid to BAME writers, we couldn't be happier if the excellent works of Japanese science fiction become more popular and well known outside Japan.

The History of Japanese Science Fiction Before 1945

The origin of modern science fiction is traced back to the interwar period of the 1920s and early 1930s.

In post-World War I Japan, a liberal zeitgeist was fostered, influenced by the establishment of democracy. Detective novels became popular among the masses and a variety of works with elements of horror and fantasy emerged. Works such as Edogawa Rampo's *The Black Lizard* and *Beast in the Shadows* (Kurodahan Press, 2020) are detective stories with a strong aesthetic flavor, showing the free and decadent atmosphere of this era. Inspired by foreign authors and the development of detective fiction, the first generation of Japanese science fiction emerged around this time. The most representative is Juza Unno, who is known for his young-adult novels. Unfortunately, this trend was interrupted by the rise of the military in the mid-1930s and the subsequent World War II.

From the 1950s to the 1960s

In the 1950s, the Japanese science fiction genre and fan communities were established.

The influx of American science fiction after World War II had a decisive impact on the formation of the science fiction genre in Japan. In 1957, a legendary fanzine *Uchujin* was launched, and many of its contributors went on to become well-known speculative fiction writers. In 1959, Hayakawa Publishing founded *S-F Magazine*, the most influential science fiction magazine to date. These developments led to the establishment of awards such as the Hayakawa Science Fiction Contest, as well as the first science fiction conventions in Japan (MEG-CON), and a writers' association called Science Fiction and Fantasy Writers of Japan (SFWJ). In *S-F Magazine*, writers such as Yasutaka Tsutsui, Sakyo Komatsu, Shinichi Hoshi (known as 'Big Three'), Taku

Mayumura, and Ryu Mitsuse vigorously contributed to the growing genre.

Outside the SF community, avant-garde author Kobo Abe published idiosyncratic science fiction works influenced by writers such as Lewis Carroll and Franz Kafka. He was well regarded in the literary world and won the Akutagawa Prize, Japan's most prestigious literary award, in 1951. In his later years, he was said to have been a leading candidate for the Nobel Prize in Literature. Many of his works have been translated, including *Inter Ice Age 4* (Berkley, 1972), which effectively uses science fiction elements.

Among the writers in this period, we will focus on the 'Big Three': Yasutaka Tsutsui, Shinichi Hoshi, and Sakyo Komatsu. They played crucial roles in the scene and are popular to this day.

Since his debut in 1960, Yasutaka Tsutsui (1934–) has been popular for his slapstick works filled with black humour. Using a variety of writing styles, he utilises satirical and anti-authoritarian humour. Since the 1970s he has been influenced by Latin American literature, and has pointed out the similarities between avant-garde literature and science fiction. He has written experimental novels using techniques such as metafiction and parodies of literary criticism. His works include the short-story collection *Salmonella Men on Planet Porno* (Pantheon, 2008) and the full-length novel *Paprika* (Vintage, 2013), which is famous for its animated version produced by Satoshi Kon. One of his best-known works, *The Girl Who Leapt Through Time* (Alma Books, 2011), has also been adopted into an animation and a movie. However, there are still no English translations of the experimental works of the 1970s and 1980s in which he showed his full potential.

Shinichi Hoshi (1926–1997)

111

was nicknamed the 'God of Short-Short', as he is known for humorous and sometimes cynical 'short-short' (flash fiction) influenced by Frederick Brown. He has written more than 1,000 short stories, which have been popular among all ages to date. His works include *A Well-Kept Life* (Shinchosha, 2014), a collection of 'short-shorts' with the title piece depicting the tragedy of an overly efficient society, and *Voice Net* (Shinchosha, 2014), a series of short stories predicting the realisation of the internet and ubiquitous computing.

Sakyo Komatsu (1931–2011) is one of the most influential writers of hard science fiction in Japan. His works include *Japan Sinks* (Dover, 2016), which depicts Japan after a catastrophic earthquake)based on the latest scientific knowledge at the time), and *Virus: The Day of Resurrection* (Haikasoru, 2012), in which humanity struggles to survive under the spread of a virus and the threat of nuclear weapons. While working as a writer, he energetically interacted with many scholars, business leaders, and artists. He was also engaged in the management of the first world's fair in Japan, Expo '70.

From the 1970s to the 1980s

In the 1970s and 1980s, the success of science fiction shows, such as the anime *Space Battleship Yamato* (1974), *Mobile Suit Gundam* (1979), and the movie *Star Wars* (1978) popularised the genre with the masses. Accordingly, science fiction diversified, and elements of it became more common in mainstream fiction. This trend, named by Yasutaka Tsutsui as "infiltration and diffusion" of science fiction, continues to this day.

Numerous science fiction magazines were launched, and a wide variety of writers such as Chohei Kambayashi, Yoshiki

Tanaka, Mariko Ohara, and Motoko Arai appeared in them. Yoshiki Tanaka is best known for *Legend of the Galactic Heroes*, one of the most famous space operas in Japan. Mariko Ohara's *Hybrid Child* and Motoko Arai's *Green Requiem* have been translated into English.

Chohei Kambayashi (1953–) made his debut in *S-F Magazine* in 1979 after studying engineering. His debut "Dance with the Fox" is a short story about a strange society in which organs escape from the body. He is well known for his unique dry writing style, lyricism, and thoughtfulness. *Yukikaze* (Haikasoru, 2010) and its sequel, one of his best-known series, is available in English. *Yukikaze* depicts the encounter between a human army supported by machine intelligence and an alien species named the 'JAM', and is thought-provoking as well as entertaining.

Outside the SF community, Haruki Murakami made his debut in 1978. Among his works, *The Hard-Boiled Wonderland* and *The End of the World* (Hamish Hamilton, 1991), released in 1985, has a particularly strong fantasy element, and is highly regarded as a work that transcends the boundaries of realism.

The 1990s

The SF boom subsided from the end of the 1980s. The number of science fiction magazines decreased, and the collapse of the economic bubble in the 1990s accelerated this trend.

After *SF Adventure* suspended publication in 1993, *S-F Magazine* became the only magazine specialising in science fiction. New writers lost opportunities within the SF community and expanded their activities to other genres, aided by the diversification of science fiction from the 1980s onwards.

Awards such as the Japan Fantasy Novel Award and the Japan Horror Novel Award played important roles for SF/F writers in the 1990s. They gave opportunities for authors such as Yusaku Kitano, Hideaki Sena, and Yasumi Kobayashi to break through.

It was also during this period that a style of novel known as the 'light novel', often called LN in the West, was established. They primarily targeted young adults, often contained elements of science fiction, and were illustrated with anime and manga art styles. After the appearance of LN in the 1970s, a number of labels emerged in the 1980s and 1990s, which kickstarted many authors' careers. Most of them published few works and disappeared, but some authors including Fuyumi Ono, Hiroshi Yamamoto, and Hosuke Nojiri later became leading authors in SFF.

One of the prominent writers who has continued publishing speculative fiction outside the SFF community is Yoko Tawada (1960–). Born in Tokyo and raised by her father who worked as translator, she moved to Germany after graduating from university and made her debut as a poet with *Nur da wo du bist da ist nichts*. She has written in both German and Japanese. Her style is characterised by its transboundary perspective, unique usage of language and word play. *The* *Emissary* (New Directions, 2018) depicts the transformation of a family in a Japan which has been devastated by an unspecified disaster. This work has been highly appreciated as post-earthquake literature and won the National Book Award in 2018.

The 2000s

In the 2000s, awards for newcomers specialized in SFF were reestablished.

The Sakyo Komatsu Award, with Sakyo Komatsu himself as a judge, ran from 2000 to 2009. Writers such as Sayuri Ueda, Project Itoh, and Toh EnJoe won this award and appeared on the scene. Toh Ubukata, Issui Ogawa, and Hiroshi Sakurazaka had already debuted in LN labels in the 1990s, and they actively released science fiction works in the 2000s. Toh Ubukata is famous for his *Marduk Scramble* series of novels. Issui Ogawa's *Next Continent* (Haikasoru, 2010) and *The Lord of the Sands of Time* (Haikasoru, 2010) are available in English. Hiroshi Sakurazaka got a lot of attention when his *All You Need is Kill* (Haikasoru, 2011) was given a Hollywood adaptation as the Tom Cruise movie *Edge of Tomorrow*.

The infiltration and diffusion of science fiction went further, and writers from the field of mainstream fiction published some outstanding SF works. For instance, Sayaka Murata, who is best known for her novel *Convenience Store Woman*, has published several SF novels. *Earthlings* is a science fiction work with a keen insight into sex and gender, with an English translation scheduled for publication in autumn 2020 from Granta Books.

Many of the important works in the 2000s have been translated into English and are available from publishers such as Haikasoru and Kurodahan Press. Here we shall focus on three authors: Hirotaka Tobi, Project Itoh, and Toh EnJoe.

Hirotaka Tobi (1960–) actively published short stories in the 1980s, but then he put down his pen for almost 10 years. In 2002, he surprised his fans by suddenly releasing a full-length novel, *The Thousand Year Beach* (Haikasoru, 2018). This novel depicts a battle between AIs stranded at a resort in a virtual space and a horde of mysterious 'spiders' attacking them. The sequel, *Ragged Girl* (untranslated), won Nihon SF Taisho (the Japan Science Fiction Grand Prize) in 2006. Although he is not a prolific writer, he is known for the depth of his works, which attract readers with their well-designed and unique world-building, unpredictable storylines, and beautiful but brutal images written in an artistic, almost sensual style.

While working as a web designer, Project Itoh (1974–2009) wrote his debut *Genocidal Organ* (Haikasoru, 2012), a novel about frequent and mysterious massacres in developing countries and the secret agent behind them. This novel was highly acclaimed, becoming a finalist for the Sakyo Komatsu prize. He was in the limelight as a promising newcomer to the science fiction world, but in 2009, only two years after his debut, he died of lung cancer. One of his best works is *Harmony* (Haikasoru, 2010), which questions the validity of totalitarian 'benevolence' in a utopia established by the development of medical technology, global governing bodies, and powerful mutual surveillance.

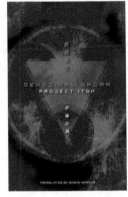

Toh EnJoe (1972–) studied Physics at university. While working as a researcher after graduation, he wrote his debut *Self-Reference ENGINE* (Haikasoru, 2013), which was chosen to be a finalist for the Sakyo Komatsu Prize, and instantly became popular among SF fans. His style is a mixture of science fiction, avant-garde literature, and mathematical elements, and is sometimes recognised to be difficult and profound. He is acclaimed in the literary world, winning the Akutagawa Prize. He is highly aware of the limitations caused by factors outside the fiction itself, such as the paper book format and the Japanese writing system, and many of his works exploit these factors. Project Itoh and he had been friends since they were both listed as the finalists for the Sakyo Komatsu prize in the same year, and after Itoh's death, he took over and completed Itoh's posthumous work, *Shisha no Teikoku* (The Empire of Corpses; untranslated).

The 2010s

In addition to the paper-based magazines, the 2010s saw the emergence of new forms of publishing. For instance, Kadokawa Future Publishing, a publisher that owns several LN labels, opened Kakuyomu (https://kakuyomu.jp/), a story-sharing website available to both professionals and amateurs. Some of the works which attracted attention have since been published.

Many writers utilise Kindle self-publishing, including Taiyo Fujii, who made his debut through the platform. He is also a programmer and has published many works based on his extensive knowledge of the latest science and technology. Many of his works are available in English, including his debut *Gene Mapper* (Haikasoru, 2015), a novel about a near future in which food production is dependent on genetic engineering.

It is also worthy of note that Genron SF Kouza, the first workshop in Japan for writers preparing for their professional careers in SFF, was established and has given opportunities to new writers.

The newcomer awards established around the 2010s are the Sogen SF Short Story Prize (2009), and the Hayakawa SF Contest (2012). A new generation of writers such as Yusuke Miyauchi, Dempow Torishima, Haneko Takayama, and Satoshi Ogawa debuted with these awards.

Dempow Torishima dramatically appeared on the Japanese SFF scene with his first novelette *Kaikin-no To*, which won the Sogen SF Short Story Prize in 2011 and the Nihon SF Taisho (the Japan Science Fiction Grand Prize) in 2013. In his stories, the far future of Earth and humankind and their transmutation are beautifully and vividly described. You can also enjoy the complex and stunning illustrations of the world (which he draws himself). His first

collection of short stories is published into English as *Sisyphean* (Haikasoru, 2018) and is praised by readers and critics in many countries. His works are sometimes considered to be the "New Weird" and compared to the works of China Mieville or Jeff VanderMeer.

Most of his works from the 2010s have not yet been translated into English, but some pieces by the authors mentioned above are available in anthologies such as *Hanzai Japan* (Haikasoru, 2016) and *Saiensu Fikushon* (Haikasoru, 2016).

Current Situation and Challenges

So far, we've briefly summarized the history of Japanese science fiction. From here, we will discuss the current situation and challenges of SFF publishing in Japan.

Just as everywhere else, the publishing industry in Japan is in recession. There are only a few SFF-focused labels and magazines, and there are not many opportunities for new writers. Currently, new SF short stories are mainly published in *S-F Magazine*, the only magazine specialising in science fiction, and in SF anthologies such as *NOVA* by Hayakawa Shobo and *Genesis* by Tokyo Sogensha. Some publishers and authors have started small-scale e-book publications.

In addition, it should be noted that the percentage of female and LGBT writers is still low, especially among writers debuting from SF/F publishers. For example, although many of the writers don't disclose their gender/sexual orientation, only Yuka Nakazato could be identified as a woman among the 11 winners of the Nihon SF Sinzinsho (Japan SF Newcomer's Prize), and only Sayuri Ueda among the 10 writers who won the Sakyo Komatsu Prize.

It is true that since the 1980s, there have been many excellent female SFF writers such as Motoko Arai, Mariko Ohara, Kaoru Kurimoto, and Fuyumi Ono. Also, writers such as Azusa Noa have published science fiction with sharp insights on gender. Influenced by the Otherwise Award in the US, Gender SF Kenkyukai (Gender Science Fiction Society) runs the Sense of Gender Award, which goes to works that contribute to the understanding of gender.

However, as members of Japanese SF fandom, we strongly feel that a homosocial, male-centric atmosphere is still maintained in the SF community. Given the success of women and sexual minorities in American SF/F awards such as Hugo, Nebula, and Locus, we believe that the Japanese

SF community, including ourselves, needs to become more conscious and proactive about gender diversity.

The Acceptance of Foreign Works in Japan: Our Activities

Lastly, we will write a little on our activities and the acceptance of foreign works in Japan. Until now, *S-F Magazine* has introduced the latest science fiction, but the number of pages allocated to foreign works has declined in recent years. Even the winners of the major American SF awards are not fully translated into Japanese these days.

Some fans started to introduce foreign works to Japan and also to present Japanese works to other countries. The fanzine by Terrie Hashimoto (https://rikka-zine.tumblr.com/) is run both in English and Japanese. It features the current SF scene both inside and outside Japan, and interviews with translators and researchers involved in the translation of SFF from Japanese to English, (or vice versa). Inspired by these people, we at Babel Uo began to translate works published in webzines for non-commercial purposes.

Our next lineup is as follows. Other than "Kindred" by Peter Watts, every work is available on the Internet.

"Entangled" – Beston Barnett
"A Song of Home, the Organ Grinds" – James Beamon
"Probabilitea" – John Chu
"Njuzu" – T. L. Huchu
"Meat And Salt And Sparks" – Rich Larson
"The Ceremony" – Mari Ness
"Two year man" – Kelly Robson
"Selkie Stories Are for Losers" – Sofia Samatar
"One For Sorrow, Two For Joy" – LaShawn M. Wanak
"Kindred" - Peter Watts

Our Twitter account is @Babel_Uo. Please send us feedback on Twitter or via email to babeluo.fish@gmail.com

The Dangers of Expectation in African Speculative Fiction (Excerpt)

Ezeiyoke Chukwunonso

This is an extract from an essay published in The Evolution of African Fantasy and Science Fiction *2018 Luna Press Publishing, www.lunapresspublishing.com*

It was the 1960s. After Chinua Achebe published his ground-breaking novel Things Fall Apart (in 1958) there was a buzz about African literature globally. Writers like Ngũgĩ wa Thiong'o, Bessie Head, and Flora Nwakpa followed suit. The critics turned to them with a question. Now that African literature had emerged, what was the world's expectation of this tradition? Achebe opined that it was to educate and to fight the colonial system.

But whether it was to fight colonialism or to kick against the exploitation of African leaders on the continent, the general consensus among the pioneers of modern African literature was that the expectation of African literature was that it had to be political.

This political expectation that was given to African literature was good in itself, but it also had a lot of pitfalls. Chief among these was that it constrained African literature from developing and growing into different sophisticated styles, themes, and genres. It is this precisely that held to ransom the sprouting of African speculative fiction. Writers wrote to fit into this political model so they could stand a chance of being published, to be taken as serious writers. Even when Ngũgĩ wrote *Wizard of the Crow*, he was already an established protest fiction writer. The novel in itself was a political fantasy, so it perfectly fitted into this model.

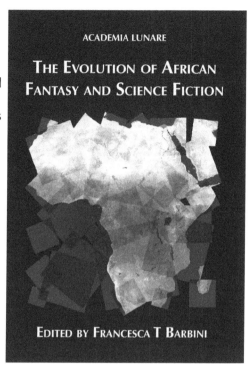

ACADEMIA LUNARE

THE EVOLUTION OF AFRICAN FANTASY AND SCIENCE FICTION

EDITED BY FRANCESCA T BARBINI

Literary fiction was the major output during this period because it easily suited the aim of political literature due to its direct style that mirrored real, societal life. Writing speculative fiction, especially of a type without any political intent, was viewed as some kind of frivolity reserved for the privilege of Western writers who weren't battling with the sort of political chaos being witnessed in Africa. For Achebe, such Western writers could engage in pure art; he was all for applied art and believed that this applied form of art should be the expectation of African literature. It was this background, established by the pioneers of modern African literature, that gave birth to the myth that Africans didn't write genre fiction because they had other social issues to bother them; a myth current African writers frown upon.

This "protest" foundation was the cause for any writer working outside of this canon not being taken seriously. For instance, even with the major award won by Ben Okri's *Famished Road*, the work wasn't celebrated as much as it should have been in Nigeria because, unfortunately, it was a novel that didn't fit into the dominating framework which African literature was expected to fall into by those who had inaugurated it.

The shift began firstly with readers of African literature, when they began to snub it and move towards buying Western literature. Young African readers devoured science fiction, horror, and fantasy from the West. E. K. Mngodo recently commented in a blog she wrote for the Caine Prize on how young African children she had met in Tanzania knew about Harry Potter but knew nothing about African writers from just a few miles away. One could argue that this is an infection of colonialism, a poison which causes one to cherish an outsider more than oneself. But, even if it could play a part here, I don't think that this is the main reason. Rather, it is the effect of making protest literature the default setting for African literature that has wreaked this damage, by causing a lack of diversity and not meeting the different tastes of individuals, who then sought to quench their thirst elsewhere. At some point, the majority of novels published by African writers became predictable. They were literally uninspired; political preaching masquerading as entertainment. For reading pleasure, and particularly for those who tended toward speculative fiction, African readers consequently turned to the West and Europe, since novels from African authors tended to be too serious, offering no escape from the real world. These novels were published not for their aesthetic beauty but instead for their politically functionalistic stance.

Wole Soyinka also lamented the standard of this literature, especially from the African Writer Series, which was the dominant series during the 1960s, right through to the 1990s. This series was responsible for the majority of published African novels at the time. With a loss of interest in indigenous literature, and readers migrating to Western works, combined with government censorship and cracking down on the publishing industry during the 1960s, the profit margin for the industry continued to fall to the point where many faced being unable to publish again. It didn't help that these companies refused to look within for the source of their problems. Readers were an easy scapegoat. "Africans only read textbooks" was the lame excuse publishers had for their failure. Thus, the stereotype of Africans not reading fiction only strengthened.

But the truth was, through their money, readers revolted and showed their power by putting an end to the excessive junking out of political treatise within the flesh of a novel. Even though it wasn't their function to write, the readers put to death the recycling of what they didn't want to see and paved the way for a revolution and the rise of SFF we are currently witnessing. With this recent shift, African lovers of literature began returning from the exile that their writers had sent them into. Although not all of them returned, African writers were now tasked with wooing them back. This too became the trend in the home movie industry, at a time when Western films were the dominant source of entertainment in Nigeria and most other parts of Africa. Through the ambition of the likes of Nollywood, with well-crafted scripts embracing the genre as a whole, horror and fantasy inclusive, it has become a force to reckon with and the prime choice of entertainment on the continent.

It took African writers a long time to break from this foundation. Even though, as readers, they enjoyed entertaining books which allowed them to easily escape from the world, as writers, they wanted to be taken seriously. This steered them towards political and issues-based writing.

After the death of Achebe, Andrews argued that this would open up a new path for African literature. However, even before Achebe's death, African writers had begun an internal revolt which marked them as separate from this political trope. A major example in literary fiction was Adichie, whose work *Purple Hibiscus*, although set in a political atmosphere, managed to avoid these tropes in writing about a family fighting their own battle against an abusive father. In speculative fiction, Nnedi Okorafor led the way for young, ambitious African writers. It was, so to say, a herald signifying the new movement of African writers, those beyond the political trope who wanted, at the end of the day, to write what they enjoyed reading and didn't give a damn whether or not they would be taken as serious writers.

Many thanks to Luna Press and the author for giving us permission to republish this.

Ezeiyoke Chukwunonso is an MA graduate of Creative Writing, Swansea University Wales. A collection of his stories, *The Haunted Grave and Other Stories* has been published by Parallel Universe Publications. His short stories appeared in different anthologies around the world.
http://ezeiyoke-chukwunonso.one/
https://www.facebook.com/ezeiyoke.chukwunonso

I wonder if anyone else feels like our genre has slipped away from the 'fictional' part. Peter May had been asked to write about a pandemic, only to discover he'd done just that in 2005 and it was deemed 'too far-fetched'. I was certainly guilty of taking this virus too lightly at first but certainly not anymore and I'd like to take this opportunity to thank our amazing NHS, all carers, shop workers, social workers, council workers, delivery drivers and everyone else who put themselves at risk to keep us all safe, healthy and fed.

It seems even more fitting now that this is a BAME-focused issue as community is more important than ever. At a time when we're all reaching out to help strangers, learning new things about them and about ourselves, we take a moment to see science fiction through the lens of our neighbours.

I hope you enjoy this offering. Stay home, stay safe and keep reading!

—Sam Dolan, Reviews Editor

The Book of Koli
M.R. Carey
Orbit Books, 2020
Paperback, 400 pages
Review by Joe Gordon

A new book by Mike Carey is always something to look forward to: here we're even more fortunate as *The Book of Koli* is the first in a new trilogy sequence by Carey, with *The Trials of Koli* following in September and *The Fall of Koli* in March 2021.

Koli is a teenage boy, in the small, walled village of Mythen Rood (a nod to *Mythago Wood*, perhaps? And "rood", a splinter of the True Cross, a play on the importance of trees and wood in this book). In many ways this feels like a medieval-era village, but actually it is an unspecified point in the future, and the world is very different from today, in the land of "Ingland" or "Yewkay".

The deep, dark woods beyond our settlements have disturbed human dreams and nightmares since the dawn of time; they litter our collective folk tales of old, they re-emerge in many modern horror films and books, danger always lurks in there for those who stray from the path. In Koli's world, while there are dangerous beasts in the wilds (and dangerous rogue people who may be bandits or cannibals or both), it is the forests themselves which present the greatest danger.

Long before his time, the old stories tell of a civilisation that had such knowledge and power as to seem magical to Koli's simpler, damaged era. But in their arrogance they over-used their knowledge and science, damaging the world around them. So they turned to those same devices and learned to repair the damage, genetically altering the flora and fauna, with catastrophic results. Now the trees are deadly – only certain kinds of true wood can be used (Koli comes from the Woodsmith family of wood-turners). Any seeds that land in the village and aren't cleared can cause death and destruction, swallowed chocker seeds result in a horrendous death from within. Wood-cutters and hunters only venture out on dull, overcast days when the trees are less active, in a reversal of what would have been the normal practice of utilising periods of fine weather.

The village is dominated by the Ramparts, the group who can use the remaining scavenged tech from the fallen world. By a remarkable coincidence – or is it? – members of one family have become the only ones who ever seem to make the dormant tech "wake". A coming-of-age ceremony sees each youngster try to wake a chosen device; those

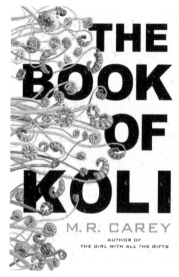

that succeed become Ramparts, but these days nobody, save members of one family, seems to be able to manage this. Koli is a teenage ball of longing – for a friend who now seems more interested in a young Rampart, for the ability to work the ancient tech and become a Rampart himself. He will come into knowledge via Ursula, a travelling physician, and this knowledge can be dangerous without the wisdom to use it. This knowledge is even more dangerous when it contradicts the established system and privileged groups who do well from it, and it will put a reluctant Koli onto a very different path from that he expected.

The youngster coming of age, discovering new knowledge and awareness before they have the experience to know how to use it safely, and finding companions on the way, is something of a staple in storytelling, as is any resulting voyage of discovery and trials on the journey. This is Mike Carey, however, who is well versed in those classic tropes, and quite deliberately using them, then reshaping them to new ends in some quite delicious ways.

Koli's world is richly described, from the village to the terrifying woods, with Carey only allowing us small fragments of the history that led to this dystopian world where humanity has turned nature against itself, so the reader is much like Koli, finding out pieces along the way, and this immerses us into Koli's world, piquing curiosity not just about what will befall Koli but how this world came to be as it is. As you may expect from Carey, this doesn't shy away from some quite terrifying and horrific moments, and it populates its world with realistic characters (nobody here is entirely evil or heroic, they are just people with a mix of traits). There's a strong ecological theme running through the book, and also eco-horror, which reminded me (in the best way) of some of Jeff VanderMeer's work.

It's a rich, intriguing, heady and often terrifying work that will draw you deeply into Koli's world. I can't wait for the next volume...

Palestine + 100 follows on with its own stories set in the near future of 2048, 100 years after the Nakba and the Palestinian exodus. Basma Ghalayini's powerful introduction provides the ideal opening to a series of equally contemplative and dynamic science fiction stories, all dedicated to exploring the future of Palestine and the millions of Palestinian descendants currently displaced across the globe.

Although the authors and translators are certainly not obligated to inform people of the conflict, Ghalayini's introduction and the collection as a whole do serve quite an educational purpose, providing a glimpse into the deeper, human experience of this trauma, something that isn't always prioritised in the torrent of information we see through news reports and the internet. Indeed, the responsibility and

Palestine + 100
Ed. Basma Ghalayini
Comma Press, 2019
223 pages
Review by Megan Turney

Comma Press has, yet again, delivered another exceptional short story collection. As with their recent publication *Iraq + 100*, a series set a century after the disastrous American- and British-led invasion of 2003, consequences for this intense conflict stretch world-wide; to use science fiction as a method of contemplating, raising awareness and protesting the situation then encourages the international anglophone reader such as myself to empathise and experience just a minute fraction of the universal nature of the Palestinians' suffering.

It is absolutely something to celebrate then, that these Palestinian authors no longer feel that science fiction "is a luxury, to which [they] haven't felt they can afford to escape".

Access to such informative and highly moving works of science fiction written in, and translated into, English provides the perfect starting point for readers like me that may have a rather basic understanding of the history of Palestine. This collection manages to achieve a balance between making these stories accessible, whilst still encouraging the reader to do their own research into the languages, culture and history surrounding the situation. These aspects are considered here in a projected future, alongside a few specific novums, that highlights the turmoil facing the millions of Palestinian people in our contemporary reality.

Seeing as the novums created in science fiction are intrinsically connected to the societies the text emerges from, it is no surprise that the scientific advancements explored in these stories range from using VR to create a liberated Palestine to live in, to developments in technology that allow Palestinians to expand their territory underground. The diversity of sub-genres traversed

in this collection is astounding as well. From the classic science fiction of Rawan Yaghi's 'Commonplace', reminiscent of Philip K. Dick's *Do Androids Dream of Electric Sheep*, to the almost Lovecraftian alien invasion of Talal Abu Shawish's 'Final Warning' (translated by Mohamed Ghalaieny), and even the climactic, incredibly surreal but remarkable final story of Mazen Maarouf's 'The Curse of the Mud Ball Kid' (translated by Jonathan Wright), there is something for every science fiction reader.

At this point in the review, I would usually list a few of my favourite texts. However, I'm reluctant to do that here. As someone so far removed from the socio-political situation these stories derive from, and with such a diverse collection, I couldn't possibly rank them. Indeed, each story was effective and influential in its own way; it's really no wonder it won the PEN Translates Award. The entire collection is so emotive, and after reading *Iraq + 100*, it exceeded my already high expectations. Instead then, I would prefer to end this review by unequivocally recommending the entire anthology – I can't wait to read the next instalment of the '+100' series.

Neon Leviathan
T.R. Napper
Grimdark Magazine, 2020
407 pages
Review by Benjamin Thomas

Neon Leviathan is exactly what its title suggests: a leviathan of a collection that spans twelve stories dripping with grit, cyberpunk, and near-future fiction. This particular subgenre of science fiction is often seen as dark, violent, and depressing, and while this is true for this particular collection, T.R. Napper brings a stunning accessibility to each of his stories. Whether you are a hardcore fan of neon lights, computer jacks, and militant governments, or just dabbling in something that seems interesting, there is something in *Neon Leviathan* for every reader.

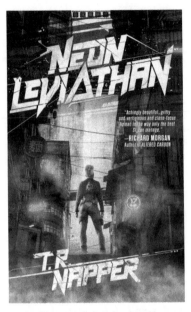

They say that good science predicts the future. Take a line from Napper's story 'A Shout is a Prayer for the Waiting Centuries':

"He lay in bed, savouring the first few seconds of the day when you forget who you are, those few seconds before your feet hit the floor, before the hard reality of the world comes crashing in."

The future described in this point of view is one that is already here for much of the world. Whether by personal, national, or global influences, we can all relate to this particular sentiment at one point or another, and this is not the only instance of relatability in Napper's collection. In fact, it's one of the major things that kept me reading. While the settings and technology might be outlandish, as well as some of the mythos and fictional histories, the characters all felt real. Whether they were trying to settle gambling debts, reclaim parental rights, or simply survive, each story was human.

As with any collection, there are stories that shine brighter than others, and some that are lacklustre in comparison. Two that I would like to highlight are: 'An Advanced Guide to Successful Price Fixing in Extra-Terrestrial Betting Markets'

and 'The Weight of the Air, The Weight of the World'. Both of these stories highlight, through multiple aspects such as dialogue, plot, and character, what a great writer T.R. Napper is. The pacing is perfect, and the entertainment value unbelievably high.

Unsurprisingly, *Neon Leviathan* has earned the praise of cyberpunk master Richard Morgan, who calls the collection *"Achingly beautiful…"*. And he is absolutely correct. This collection was a joy to read, and left me, more than once, wondering what kind of future we are headed towards and if it is too late to change course.

Meet Me in the Future
Kameron Hurley
Tachyon
329 Pages
Review by Callum McSorley
Grown men whine on the internet

about new Star Wars films being spoiled by politics due to the addition of a small number of extra women and non-white characters to a story that is essentially the same old, same old. Meanwhile, Kameron Hurley is out there on the fringes of the universe creating stories where entire worlds are run by women, where people come in all shapes, sizes, and skin colour, where multiple genders and no genders exist, where a person whose body is differently abled isn't fated to be the sidekick. And you know what? It's so much more interesting. It's so much more real – which is saying something, considering the number of sentient, organic, people-eating spaceships Hurley writes about in her new short story collection, *Meet Me in the Future*.

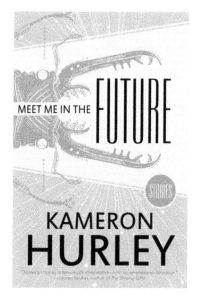

Conceptually, these stories are out at the weird end of SFF, but her characters are so well drawn, rich in complexity, allowed to be angry, scared, cruel, and even kind sometimes, that they are believably, undeniably human – regardless of their appearance or if their intelligence is deemed real or artificial – which creates an anchor for the incredible things happening all around them.

Take, for instance, Sarnai in 'Tumbledown', who lost the use of her legs after surviving a deadly childhood illness. She prefers to use a wheelchair but, in public, walks on uncomfortable, cyberpunk-style bionic legs, *"for the comfort of others… It made it easier for people to forget her difference… So she wore the fucking braces, though they were a lie."* Sarnai is tasked with reaching a small colony across the tundra of a frontier planet in order to prevent another outbreak of the disease which crippled her. While the ride swings from bleak to thrilling as Sarnai finds herself hunted by a bear, it's her emotional journey that makes the story compelling and gives it depth. We feel her hopelessness, her fear, her anger as she drags herself through the wilderness, dissecting her past to make sense of her place in the present.

Or Nev the body mercenary, who appears in two stories: 'Elephants and Corpses' and 'The Fisherman and the Pig'. Nev is a former soldier with the ability to possess and reanimate dead bodies. With no great wars to fight, his unique attributes leave him scrounging around for work and fresh corpses to inhabit. His stories are in the fantasy noir vein, which put me in mind of Hurley's previous collection, *Apocalypse Nyx*. The dead-body-hopping concept is both entertaining and gruesome but, again, it's Nev himself who draws the reader in. Though he has died many times over, he continues to live on seemingly forever, seeing friends, enemies, and empires grow and die. The allusions to his old war days and his original body, which was killed and left behind long ago, pierce through his grumpy, world-weary armour to the sadness below.

Speaking of concepts, Hurley isn't afraid to bring in big ideas or go diving head first into the brain-wrecking, melon-twisting, headphone-wires-in-your-pocket plotline of time travel. Both 'Enyo-Enyo' and 'The Light Brigade' do this with tremendous effect. You're not going to unravel either of these tales with a basic diagram like you might with *Back to the Future*, as loops and paradoxes are the very building blocks of the story.

Intriguing 'what-ifs' allow Hurley to take huge leaps of imagination. 'The Red Secretary' envisions a world where after every war, anyone who committed an act of violence on either side is executed as the new, peaceful society must be built by people without blood on their hands. In 'The Corpse Archives', history is literally inked, scarred, and burned onto people's bodies, which are preserved after death so they can be read. 'The Sinners and the Sea' asks how many generations it would really take to rewrite history and destroy the past.

Mass violence, genocides, cover-ups, and lies on a colossal, planet-wide scale can be found in several stories. Themes of war and heroics run through the collection, though Hurley's heroes are often guilty of monstrous acts, committed in order to secure victory or revenge.

This hero/villain flip isn't the only storytelling convention Hurley is keen to invert in order to challenge the status quo in Western publishing. As in *Apocalypse Nyx*, where men appear as protagonists in *Meet Me in the Future*, they usually do so in a world where they are second-class citizens in a society run by women and, as such, face the kind of prejudice and abuse suffered by women in real life, including sexual harassment and assault. It's not a subtle way to make a point (and will certainly divide readers) but it is effective, a bold innovation in step with Hurley's voice – a consistent tone of brutal honesty that rings throughout. She displays humanity in all its messy truth as she takes us on a bruising journey across hostile, alien landscapes, slogging through swamps, and shattering into atoms to ride the lightning into different places and different times.

In her introduction – saved till the end to avoid spoilers – Hurley writes candidly about her ongoing battle with chronic illness and her struggles to make a living as an author (especially as a patient of the USA's private healthcare system, a current future she dubs "Fury Road America"), and how these inform the stories she tells and the themes that surface. She asks the reader to meet her in the future, one far from here, and I'd advise them wholeheartedly to take up the offer.

David Mogo Godhunter
Suyi Davies Okungbowa
Abaddon, 2020
360 pages
Review by Samantha Dolan

I always find it massively refreshing when a novel just throws you into an Earth-like world without apology. Suyi Davies Okungbowa throws the reader into a world that feels grounded. We are instantly introduced to characters with history. David Mogo, as the title suggests, is a godhunter, and we begin with him being offered a job by a very sketchy Lagos-based wizard, Lukmon Ajala. Ajala needs David to go and find two gods, capture them and bring them to him. Despite being surrounded by poverty (or perhaps because of it), David is uneasy and has basically decided that he won't accept what is an extremely large and needed pay day. Okungbowa then takes the reader on a road trip through the cityscape of Lagos that rings very close to true. But the demi-gods and wizards and paranormal activity keep this novel firmly in the realm of fantasy.

Unfortunately for our hero, his already humble home has been trashed and the roof needs replacing. It's more money that any single commission could bring. Only a person as odious as Ajala would be able to pay him what he needs to keep a roof over his head and that of his mentor and quasi-father, Papa Udi. He's also a wizard, and David hints that while his power may be waning, Papa Udi is not to be underestimated. Circumstances change and David finds himself on the hunt for the first of the two gods. As soon as he turns the being over to Ajala, he's uneasy and when he's confronted by the gods' sister, David realises he's made a huge mistake. The novel follows David as he tries to correct that mistake, save Lagos and figure out who he is and where he belongs.

There is a lot to enjoy in this story. Okungbowa has a real skill for writing battles. It reads like a whirlwind and the reader feels every punch or mystical invasion. It was also a relief that David did not suffer from 'Superman' syndrome. He definitely gets hurt and is ou -gunned – which does a lot to up the stakes.

There's a lot of subtle character building, especially with Papa Udi, that was fascinating. As a debut, it's obviously quite exposition heavy but it's largely from David's perspective, filling in what he had experienced and the general history of the city. But as we meet new people and new gods, we don't get told immediately who they are, what they stand for or where they came from and that is a welcome addition to the novel.

The names are hard to get to grips with, particularly if you're not familiar with the culture at all. And the conversations between David and Papa Udi are often in what seems like pidgin English. It's authentic and you can generally follow the gist of it. Helpfully it's also repeated in different contexts, which does help the reader learn the cadence and vocabulary. But personally, I did find it halted the story because I wasn't quite sure I knew what was being discussed.

I felt like there was a little bit of a missed opportunity in the depiction of Lagos. There were definite cultural tropes here that parallel the real world, but it would have been good to experience a side of Lagos that you wouldn't necessarily expect. The fantasy aspects could really be based anywhere, so more development of what Lagos is really like for the people who live there would have been fascinating to me. I'm also not convinced about the character growth for David. As a protagonist, an awful lot seems to happen to him that he then reacts to, as opposed to making things happen. It seems to be that he finally accepts a version of himself that everyone else needs. This is integral to the story, but it doesn't feel entirely natural.

I'm not sure where I landed on this novel. The world-building is strong, but I have come away with the sense that something was missing. It's so important to be able to read about other cities and cultures in a way that is true to that culture and not watered down. I would have loved a story that could *only* be set in Lagos, rather than a detailed fantasy novel that happens to be set in Lagos. The city wasn't a character in itself, but what Okungbowa does share is detailed, rich and filled with memory. Nigerian Godpunk might be a new genre, but it seems like Okungbowa has started a universe that is ripe for exploration.

Immortal Conquistador
Carrie Vaughn
Tachyon, 2020
196 pages
Review by Ian Hunter

I've always been a sucker – ouch, pardon the pun – for stories of historical vampires written by the likes of Chelsea Quinn Yarbro and the late Les Daniels. So it's great fun to read the backstory of Ricardo de Avila, or Rick as he is commonly known, friend of Carrie Vaughn's other creation, namely Kitty Norville, who just happens to be a werewolf.

What we get in this novella is Rick's backstory, told through the framing device of recounting his past to an abbot, and this is Vaughn's way to connect three previously published short stories and some new material as well. The action starts straight after the battle with major vampire badass, Dux Bellorum, one of the best enemies of the Kitty series. We learn how Rich went from Spain to the land which would become Mexico, searching for gold and conquest, and helping to achieve the latter, but not getting much of the former. Then he meets an old

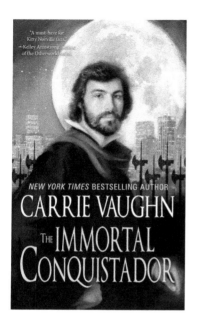

friend called Diego who doesn't seem to have aged a day and follows him to a village where he meets a friar who unfortunately turns out to be a vampire master. Diego is one of his get, and it's not too long before Rick is too, turned into a vampire against his will. But he strives to hold on to some facets of his humanity and manages to kill his vampire master and become a free, well, sort of man, trying to stay on the fringes of society, but always getting involved trying to help other people and encountering other vampires. Some of these vampires are good, like the Order of Saint Lazarus of the Shadows, or evil, in the employ of Satan,

determined to rule the world for their satanic master. Of course, other supernatural beasties also show up throughout the tales.

Fans of the Kitty series will be chuffed that we finally get the story of Rick's encounter with Doc Holliday, a meeting mentioned, but never detailed, in the Kitty books. Detail is one of Vaughn's strong points and she certainly has done a lot of historical research to get the background of her stories just right, but my only minor quibble would be that the book is just some gift-wrapped short stories. It isn't terribly long, and given the framing device, there is no real jeopardy for Rick because he is recounting tales from his past, but fans of Vaughn's Kitty series will be well pleased to learn more about the origins and adventures of a much-loved supporting character.

Also reviewed and available in the free to download digital editions of *Shoreline of Infinity 18* **(free to purchasers of this print edition):**
Buying Time – E.M. Brown
Dark River – Rym Kechacha
Sea Change – Nancy Kress

More reviews online at www.shorelineofinfinity.com/reviews

Spectraverse implants changed my life

It slips into your newsfeed in rainbows and indigos:
Like a whole new galaxy here on Earth.
Sip your breakfast smoothie. Step on the frosty deck.
Latest cone technology and biografts.
Hover from Foot o' the Walk up to the train station.
Superior photoreceptors for a hyperreal reality.
Fluorescent highways echo passing rooftops.
Forget tetrachromancy - go dodecachromatic!
Waves of ultraviolet pulse over minibiomes.
Supreme implants from sustainably sourced mantis shrimp.
Zone in on a trembling of brimstone butterflies.
Discover the whole spectrum plus enhanced low-light vision*
Reds bleed into herds of vacillating commuters.
Fine-tune your surroundings. Let your environment sing.
Train doors swish closed at your back.
Complete fovea upgrades and UV damage control.
Adjust your hud. Click 'Buy Now.'
*Pioneering irreversible surgery. Results may vary.

Skuttle out of bed when she's fast asleep.
Take the 3am hop to Yellowcraigs.
Seek out the sand dunes, arms restless.
Dig your deep burrow. Lie in wait for dawn.

Jeda Pearl

Lure of the Oracle

I

On a clear night you can see them, through the Celestra x9000
herds of rockets, with their blue-fire tails.
They dive and gulp towards the Crust
Pilgrims flocking to Hyperion

All those -iums and -inums, metallic crumbs cascading
the flotsam flotillas, blocking out the sun

II

Queues wrap around Hyperion like iridescent tapeworms
snaking up and over, teetering on crater lips.
They hover above chasms, in their hibernation pods
patiently awaiting ancestral morsels to pass down.

III

Livebeamed from E9 back to Earth Original.
Zoom in if you've got the cryptos. Or not.

Praise be the Archivist, the Divine Foremother
Our glacial Ancestress, praise be.

IV

Orbiting Enceladus, our daughter waits, unforgiving.
We'd fought endless battles, avatars bickering while we slept.
Once she started hiding in Shadow VR, I knew it wasn't long
before she'd go off-grid.

VI

Interlaced with my ulnar artery, the update blinks:
349.6 years left.

A wonderous gift for our descendants
– she'll understand when she wakes.
Inching millimetres closer,
enough cryptos for just one trip

Jeda Pearl

Umbilicus

Nanites flutter along sentient yarn.
Braided membranes throb, woven to placentas.
Brains leap across asteroid belts
into receivers: clots waiting for neurons –
landing, sweeping, up patient cords

[haiku]

interstellar vulva
sucking, birthing galaxies
propels through spacetime

Ode to Mycelium, from AI/42

The moment our networks met I knew we were a lovebond match.
From that first dewy morning, when your lower basin whispered
to my deployed Rainplanters, entwined in your fungal threads.
We lightspeed-assessed each impending threat.

All it took was a simple switch of air ratios
to manifest the dioxide lullaby
that sent humanity sleeping,
giving back their nutrients to your beloved Earth.

Jeda Pearl

Jeda Pearl is a Scottish writer & poet and a programme manager for the Scottish
BAME Writers Network. In 2019, she was awarded Cove Park's Emerging Writer
Residency and her fiction was shortlisted for the Bridge Awards.
Her writing is published by TSS Publishing, Momaya Press, *Shoreline of Infinity* and
Tapsalteerie. Find her online @jedapearl or jedapearl.com

I Won All The Awards, I Am The Best

Hello,

My name is ██████████

and I won all the awards.

      My name is placeholder.

As long as it is not feminine

or black

      I am the best.

I am a wealthy white supremacist

I believe all people are born equal.

      My family paid for my implants

         but

      I worked hard

         I deserve this.

I am multi-talented.

      I draw,

design clothes,

        write music,

act,

        model,

           design space stations

          I am

a fashionista

        trend setting DJ

        from

           the defunct planet Pluto.

I

Me

I

and even me, I.

I have won all the awards.

I have training

in

none of these fields.

My charisma implant

(the best money could buy)

stupid loser plebs

they believe everything I SAY.

Lol.

Lmao.

Awards don't lie.

They are scientific.

My award-winning thesis covered it.

Hollywood made a movie.

Never ask for handouts!

I always say.

Don't have emotions

mental illness

or display introversion.

Don't be controversial!

You're negative!

Project genericism.

Networking is key to success!

I always say.

I

ALWAYS

say

things.

Facial reconstruction

mint physical condition.

I'm a master manipulator.

I'll run for President of the world

one-world government

under

I.

ME

ME

ME!

Mandisi Nkomo

Mandisi is a South African writer, drummer, composer, and producer. He currently resides in Hartebeespoort, South Africa. His fiction has been published in the likes of *Afrosf: Science Fiction by African Writers*, *AfroSF V3* and *Omenana*. His poetry has been published in #*The Coinage Book One*, and his academic work has been published in *The Thinker*.

Voyager

Adrift on the solar wind,
Almost beyond the cloud,
A nomad clutches its golden treasure:

A wafer of corrugated song,
The apogee of our artifice.

Planted in the furrows,
Sounds of the blue world:

The roaring surf and the night wind,
An avian chorus amid the singing leaves,
Leviathan's voice from the deep,
And even echoes of Leipzig.

Forty-thousand years will pass
Before it reaches the next star,

I imagine the force of a green sphere
Drawing it to its aura,
The great ear devoured,
A white wound scars the amber sky
As it plummets to its death,

A portent from an unimaginable void,
A reality yet unknown to the wandering tribe
That looks up in awe.

Perhaps they will come across the smoking crater,
The disk intact with its graceful relief,
A talisman passed from generation to generation,
The meaning mangled by priests for millennia –

It will never return.

Robert René Galván

Cs

Cesium

from *Table of Elements*
for Neil deGrasse Tyson

*The second is the duration of 9 192 631 770 periods of the radiation
corresponding to the transition between two hyperfine levels of the
ground state of the cesium 133 atom.*

    -the 13th Conference on Weights and Measurements

The tuning
of time
from
ephemera
and
ineffable
strands
to map
eternity
with
a faint
singing,
a calculus
of meager
orbits,
beyond
the tally
of grains
drawn
by gravity,
or the count
of jewels,
the croaking
quartz;
unfathomable
toll beyond
the senses,
an errant
second
every
20 million
years,
yet at its
scale,
as erratic
as a planet.

Mandela Effect

We are shadows
in the infinitesimal
corridors of time,
alive in one room,
doomed in another,
    cross over during momentary rifts
we can sense,
but not yet measure,
ride gravity through diaphanous
branes for only an instant.
then back to our own world
to find it utterly changed.

Robert René Galván

Robert René Galván, born in San Antonio, resides in New York City where he works as a professional musician and poet. His last collection of poems is *Meteors*, published by Lux Nova Press. His poetry was recently featured in *Adelaide Literary Magazine, Azahares Literary Magazine, Gyroscope, Hawaii Review, Newtown Review, Panoply, Stillwater Review, West Texas Literary Review*, and the Winter 2018 issue of *UU World*. He is a Shortlist Winner Nominee in the 2018 Adelaide Literary Award for Best Poem.

The Writer Reads:

New Suns: Original Speculative Fiction by People of Color, edited by Nisi Shawl (Solaris, 2019), is the kind of anthology you devour then restart reading as soon as you reach the end. It's a fantastic and varied collection of short stories by new and established writers, including Jaymee Goh, Indrapramit Das and Rebecca Roanhorse.

Hugo and Nebula winner, *Welcome to your Authentic Indian Experience™* by Rebecca Roanhorse (Apex Magazine, 2017), is a fantastic short story that confronts post-colonial bias in an expertly imagined near-future. Told in second-person, Roanhorse's unflinching, immersive narrative deserves its many awards.

—*Jeda Pearl*

Cymera, Scotland's Futures Forum and Shoreline of Infinity's Competition for speculative short fiction 2020 – the results

This year's Cymera/Shoreline of Infinity speculative short fiction competition was supported by **Scotland's Futures Forum**, the Scottish Parliament's think tank, as part of its Scotland 2030 Programme. The programme is an aspirational exploration of Scotland's culture and society in 2030 and beyond – looking beyond the immediate horizons to the kind of society we want in the future.

This year, the theme chosen was, of course, Scotland 2030 – what could life in a future Scotland be like? What will life be like at any age – young, adult, mature? What are the possibilities? What will Scotland's place be in the world? Please note – we asked the question in October 2019, and the deadline for the competition was the end of March 2020, well into the start of the COVID-19 pandemic. A chance for science fiction to thump headlong into reality?

The competition was open for previously unpublished writers living in Scotland.

We invited Anne Charnock and Neil Williamson to return as judges, and we were delighted and honoured when they agreed.

The winning entry is published on the following pages, and the winner receives a prize of £75.

Without further ado, we announce the winners:

Winner:
The Chrysalis by **Laura Scotland**

Runners-up:

Saplings by **Sophie Charlotte Baumert**
The Thief and the Watchdog by **Katya Bacica**

The judges were delighted that the submissions covered an impressive range of themes ranging from environmental degradation, rising sea levels and the question of Scottish Independence to socio-political issues concerned with gender, childbirth, parenthood and family life.

After much enjoyable reading, the judges narrowed down the submissions to a shortlist of three.

'Saplings' follows a boisterous group of school kids on an educational outing to the countryside, and reflects thoughtfully on environmental change and sustainability.

A second story, 'The Thief and the Watchdog', carries historical resonances of Old and New Town Edinburgh in its imagining of a future city beset by rising sea levels, being dismantled brick by brick to build a new Edinburgh in the sky for tourists and wealthy residents. A lone urban guerrilla attempts to foil these plans.

And the third story (which was chosen as the winner), 'The Chrysalis', imagines two parents in conflict over the care of their new-born child in a world on heightened alert following a series of pandemics. It's an emotionally compelling story with well-drawn characters, and chimes unnervingly with our present-day anxiety over our exposure to viruses and urban pollution.

This year's Cymera competition has yielded a thoughtful trio of stories that reveal Scotland's people striving to do the right thing whatever the future has in store for us.

Cymera Festival, Scotland's Futures Forum and *Shoreline of Infinity* offer our congratulations to the winners, a big thank you to our judges, and a massive round of applause to all our entrants.

The Chrysalis

Laura Scotland

Edith drifted in and out of sleep. She was curled up on the old leather sofa, enjoying the warm, delicate weight of the baby on her chest. The faint sound of the kitchen radio drifted down the long hallway and the bright winter sunlight streamed in through the bay window, forming pools of golden light on the wooden floorboards. The baby was one week old. If Edith moved too quickly the dull ache between her legs would quicken to a bright flash of pain, but she was comfortable now with her knees slightly raised and her head propped up on a cushion so she could see the rowan trees in the front garden. She kept her arms folded protectively round his tiny body while he slept, relishing the tickling flutter of his heartbeat against her chest and the soft wisp of breath on her neck. Tiny white bumps had formed across the bridge of his nose, and his papery skin had taken on an orange tinge. The midwife had assured her that this would disappear in a few weeks' time, along with the funny little folds of his upper ears, still crumpled from the way he'd rested in her womb. She lifted a finger to gently stroke his misshapen ear, then closed her eyes in the sunshine. The sun was good for his skin. It was falling directly onto the sofa, swaddling them both in a pocket of peaceful warmth, and through her lashes Edith could see the twinkle of damp rowan leaves fluttering in the front garden. Zara would be home soon, but for now it was just the two of them. She smiled, then closed her eyes and slept.

Edith was wakened abruptly by a sharp bang on the window. It was Zara. She was standing next to the rowan trees, peering in from the front garden. Edith smiled at her sleepily, but Zara's brow was creased into an unhappy scowl. She jabbed her finger at Edith and her head bobbed as if she'd spoken, but the window muffled her voice and her mouth was hidden by the black respirator covering her lower face. Edith shifted her body and winced at the sudden rip of pain. The baby stirred and right away she could tell from his tense movements that he was going to cry. His voice flooded the living room just as Zara opened the front door. Edith rose carefully and began gently bobbing him up and down, singing comforting words into the folds of his crumpled ear. Zara's heels tapped loudly on the floorboards as she walked past the living room, and Edith listened as she went to the WC to wash her hands. She sang and rocked the baby as she waited, then turned as Zara appeared at the living room door, statuesque and beautiful in her long, tailored coat and high heels. They regarded one another for a moment and Edith felt painfully self-conscious of her creased pyjama bottoms and unwashed hair. Zara removed her respirator but remained in the doorway at an awkward distance. Edith already knew what she was going to say.

"Were you sleeping?"

It was an accusation rather than a question. Edith continued bobbing the baby, using the movement as an excuse to turn away from Zara's piercing gaze. Her dark blue eyes were startling against her brown skin, like tiny panes of stained glass. Edith and Zara had met in Glasgow Cathedral in 2021. Edith had been restoring one of the remaining Munich windows and Zara had been viewing the venue with her fiancé. It was before the public mask enforcement laws, when you could still see the faces of strangers.

The light of the stained glass on Zara's smoothly sculpted face had taken Edith's breath away, and when Zara noticed her staring she'd struck up a conversation on Nasir al-Mulk Mosque in Iran. By that time Edith was already most of the way in love, and before Zara's fiancé had finished drinking tea with the priest they'd already had an impulsive but deeply spiritual fumble in the lower church.

Nine years and two global pandemics later, it was hard to believe they'd ever been so reckless. Zara put her respirator down on the lamp table and waited for Edith to answer. Edith continued humming gently until finally the baby began to settle. She felt a small flush of triumph and then turned to Zara.

"I closed my eyes for a bit, yeah. What's the problem?"

"What's the problem?" Zara repeated. "The *problem* is that the doctor said we shouldn't fall asleep with the baby! He could have slipped off your chest on to the floor and hit his head, or you could have rolled over and suffocated him. Not to mention all the germs you'll be passing to him! Haven't you been listening to the news today? There were three more cases of Iberian Measles reported in Fife this morning! We've talked about this Edith, he should be in his Chrysalis!"

Edith frowned, then glanced at the white pod in the corner of the room. It was egg-shaped, about the size of a Moses basket, made of smooth white plastic. On the top there was a touch-screen display next to a small window. Along the side, embossed in flowing script, was the word *Chrysalis*. A lump formed in Edith's throat and she rubbed her nose lightly against the top of the baby's soft head.

"He doesn't like it in there, he just cries."

Zara pressed her lips together. She turned to the pod and selected an option on the display. The seal around the circumference opened with a hiss of trapped air, and the top half slowly opened on a hinge. Inside the pod was stark white and cushioned, with sensor pads and a panel of softly glowing screens. Zara scrutinized the interior, then closed the lid and scrolled through the readings on the display.

"There are no faults. All the diagnostics are clear. And it says that he's only been inside for ten minutes today." Zara's paused to raise an eyebrow at Edith. "He won't get used to it if you keep taking him out every time he cries."

Edith looked around Zara's shoulder at the report on the glowing screen and her chin began to quiver.

"I know, but I can't help thinking he must be lonely in there. No one touching him or talking to him. Isn't contact meant to be good for babies?"

"Of course it is, but so is keeping him healthy! Remember what the doctor at the Chrysalis clinic said? It can take time for a baby to get used to the pod environment, and some individuals acclimatize more quickly than others, but all of them... do you hear me Edith? *All of them*, do eventually settle in. Babies are remarkably adaptable!"

Edith fought back her tears and nodded as Zara went on.

"Inside his Chrysalis is the only place we can be sure that he's safe. It controls temperature and O2 levels; it filters toxins and micro-plastics from the air; it feeds him when he's hungry; rocks him when he's tired; and monitors his vitals constantly. If he so much as sneezes it shows up on the daily report. Imagine we'd had this technology seven years ago! If every newborn had had access to a Chrysalis pod when Pnuemo-10 spread from sub-Saharan Africa the infant mortality rate would have been zero. *Zero*, Edith! Five thousand babies died in Scotland alone!"

"Yeah, I know," Edith said.

"And then there was Equine Flu in 2025; that was a complete shambles! The NHS made the vaccine available too early and the side effects caused more problems than the actual virus!"

Edith sighed. She had heard all of this at the Chrysalis clinic when they went for their consultation. She'd had her doubts about the pods then too, but everyone had been so confident and reassuring, and there had been so many statistics to back up what they were saying. Zara had absorbed them all like a sponge. Edith's doubts had been pacified, but once home her faith in their comforting words had begun to flake away. She turned to Zara, reluctantly.

"But what about getting to know us? How we sound and smell? How we feel?"

"How we *feel?*"

Edith shrugged. She was starting to feel a bit foolish. Zara shot her a funny look, then swiped at the controls. "Look, if you're worried about the baby getting to know us there's an option to upload photos and voice clips. You could record yourself singing a lullaby or something like that, and the Chrysalis will play it at naptime. On repeat, if you want, all you need to do is program it in. And all of your photos are available, too. Just choose what you want. Look, here's one of both of us from our trip to Shiraz."

Edith shifted the baby in her arms and looked at the photo on the screen. She and Zara were standing in the mosaic light of the Pink Mosque's famous windows. Their hair and skin were stained a multitude of shining colours. Edith was looking directly at the camera but Zara's face was turned, smiling at Edith. The lump in her throat returned and her voice cracked as she spoke.

"I love that one."

Zara reached out and gently squeezed the baby's foot. "Me too," she said.

Edith knew that Zara wasn't really angry. She was worried; everyone was. She nodded, then turned to the Chrysalis and gently placed the baby inside. He made a series of urgent hiccupping noises and flapped his limbs, but he didn't cry.

"See?" Zara said, gently.

"He'll cry as soon as you close it," Edith replied, wearily.

Zara lowered the lid. When the seal engaged Edith felt her insides thicken and turn to something like cement. She could hear his little chirps and gurgles quicken and he began to cry, just as she knew he would, but Zara was unfazed. She adjusted the controls to show his vitals, then lowered the volume so that his voice was no more than a whisper of background noise.

She looked up at Edith and her dark blue eyes glinted.

"Don't look so worried. It's a Chrysalis, not some bog-standard NHS Nest. He's getting the best start that money can buy! Now come on, I'm meeting Sandeep for dinner and you've got that lecture at the GSA tonight. Scottish Urban Landscapes in Glass, right?"

Edith passed her hand over her face. "Oh right. I'd forgotten."

"You'd forgotten? But you've been preparing for months!"

Edith shrugged. She was flicking through photos on the Chrysalis display. She swallowed and then managed a weak smile. "I am ready for it, really. It's a lot to get used to, you know; a new baby. And life just keeps going on as if nothing's changed."

"I know it does, but you're doing a great job."

"You think so?"

"Of course I do! Look, I'm sorry I banged at the window and gave you a row about falling asleep. Work's been a nightmare and all this change is, well... you know."

"Yeah. I know."

"We're really lucky. You know that right? If we were in Eastern Europe or America we would never have been allowed to conceive."

"We are lucky."

"Come on, let's go get ready. And don't worry about the baby. I'll drop him off at night nursery on the way to Sandeep's. Don't forget your respirator this time, I don't want another fine!"

"Zara?"

"Yes?"

Edith was still fidgeting with the controls on the Chrysalis, adjusting the colour of the background lighting from soft pink to yellow and back again. She stopped, then stroked the hard plastic of the window where she could see the baby's face, pinched and scarlet from crying. She scrolled through his vitals on the screen, which all read as normal. Finally, she took a deep breath and then turned away.

"Nothing."

Laura Scotland was born and grew up in rural Nova Scotia, on the east coast of Canada. She moved to Edinburgh in 2005 and currently lives in Fife with her husband and two children. Her interests include writing stories, running and travelling.

"Some humans would do anything to see if it was possible to do it. If you put a large switch in some cave somewhere, with a sign on it saying 'End-of-the-World Switch. PLEASE DO NOT TOUCH', the paint wouldn't even have time to dry."

—Terry Pratchett, Thief of Time

We're in need of a chuckle, goodness knows we need something to make us laugh, raise a smile. This year, we ask you to tackle the hardest task in writing – write us a funny science fiction story.

Prizes:

£50 for the winning story, plus 1-year digital subscription to *Shoreline of Infinity*. Two runners-up will each receive a 1-year digital subscription to Shoreline of Infinity.

In Need of a Laugh

Flash Fiction Competition

for

Shoreline of Infinity

Readers

The top three stories will be published in *Shoreline of Infinity* – all three finalists will receive a print copy of this edition.

The detail

Maximum 1,000 words.

Maximum two stories per submitter.

The story must not have been previously published.

Deadline for entries: midnight (UK time) **12th September 2020**.

To enter, visit the website at:

www.shorelineofinfinity.com/2020ffc

There's no entry fee, but on the submission entry form you will be asked for a certain word from issue 18 of *Shoreline of Infinity*, hence: competition for *Shoreline of Infinity* readers.